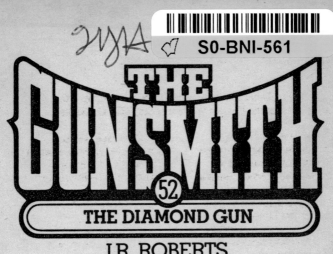

THE GUNSMITH

52

THE DIAMOND GUN

J.R. ROBERTS

CHARTER BOOKS, NEW YORK

THE GUNSMITH #52: THE DIAMOND GUN

A Charter Book/published by arrangement with
the author

PRINTING HISTORY
Charter edition/April 1986

ISBN: 0-441-30956-9

Charter Books are published by The Berkley Publishing Group,
200 Madison Avenue, New York, New York 10016.
PRINTED IN THE UNITED STATES OF AMERICA

To Matthew Joseph Randisi
b. 12:42 p.m., 7/25/85
7 pounds, 10 ounces

ONE

As Clint Adams directed his rig and team down the main street of the town of Flint, Colorado, about twenty miles from the New Mexico border, his mind was wandering to past places, people, and experiences, both good and bad. A montage of people flicked across his consciousness—friends, enemies, lovers, acquaintances. Among them was a man named Dan Rondo. Well, now his name was Dan Rondo, but once it had been Ron Diamond, better known as the Diamond Gun.

Clint grimaced at the thought of Diamond's nickname—or perhaps he was grimacing at his own nickname, his own curse—the Gunsmith.

Well, at least Diamond had outrun the name and had settled into a small New Mexico town. He was married now, he had a business of his own, and, for all Clint knew, he could even have a kid by now.

Clint Adams had long ago given up the hope of ever having a life like that. No, that wasn't true. He'd never had such a hope. In fact, he didn't think that he would be able to sit still for such a life because he had a problem doing that little thing—sitting still.

All of this had gone through Clint's mind in a second, and then his mind had moved on to other names, other faces. He had no idea that in a short time he would be meeting up with

1

Ron Diamond again—not Dan Rondo, but Ron Diamond, the Diamond Gun.

Delores Rondo missed her husband.

Dan Rondo had taken a wagon loaded with supplies out of town early the morning before, and he was supposed to return tonight—actually, within a few hours. Knowing that he would be home soon made her miss him all the more. If her father hadn't died a few months back, it might have been different; she might not have felt so lonely, but as it was now, she couldn't wait for her husband to come back.

Delores was in her early twenties; her husband was close to fifty. The difference in their ages made no difference to her, however. He was a kind man, a good provider, a satisfying lover. He loved her very much. That was all any woman could ask of a husband.

Delores was in the general store that they owned and operated. She had been running it alone for the days Dan was gone. When two men entered the store, she looked at them as simply two more customers.

She had no idea that they would be the last two customers she would ever serve.

Dan Rondo was on his way back to Canaan, New Mexico, where Deolores and his store were waiting. For the hundredth, or maybe the thousandth time, he counted his blessing that a woman as young and vital as Delores could love him, could want to spend her life with him—even after she had found out about his past as Ron Diamond, gunfighter.

Something inside Dan Rondo—some small part of Ron Diamond's past, perhaps—told him that the happiness couldn't last. He'd killed too many men in his life—most of them in self-defense, but, admittedly, some when there might have been another way—for the rest of his life to be spent in such unmatched happiness.

It was only a matter of when.

"Can I help you?" Deolores asked the two men.

They were both young men, one in his late twenties, the other in his early thirties, and they looked at her the way many men looked at her. Usually, Dan was around to temper those looks—he was an impressive figure even without a gun—but he was not here today, and suddenly she was afraid.

"Well, hello, little lady," one of the men said, eyeing her hungrily.

"What are you talking about, Linc?" the younger man asked. "This here ain't no little lady. Look at the size of her . . . My, my, my."

Both men were staring at her breasts, which were large, firm, and round. It was a warm day and she had been working in the storeroom. Her perspiration had made her blouse stick to her skin. Through the fabric, they could plainly see her nipples, big as thumbs and with wide, dark brown aureoles.

"Please," she said, putting both hands on the counter, "if there is something I can help you with—"

"Well, there sure is," the man called Linc said. "We came in here for some supplies, but now there's something else I want."

He turned and looked at his friend. After they'd exchanged glances for a seemingly interminable time, the second man nodded. He turned, walked to the door, closed it, and locked it.

"Please," Delores said, "open the door."

The man by the door simply grinned and walked away from the door. Delores moved one hand off the counter and dropped it down out of sight, groping for the gun that was underneath. Dan had showed her how to use it in case of a robbery. "Let them have what they want," Dan had told her, "and don't grab for the gun unless you think they're going to hurt you."

Well, she knew what these men wanted, and she had no intention of simply letting them have it.

"All right," the man named Linc said. He started around the counter, the other man right behind him. They both had the same evil, hungry looks on their faces.

Linc approached her and she pulled the gun out from beneath the counter, but too slowly. He grabbed her wrist and held it tightly.

"Hey, this little lady's got fangs," he said, laughing. He twisted her wrist cruelly until she yelped in pain and dropped the gun to the floor.

"Well, now . . ." he said, licking his lips. With one hand still holding her wrist, he wrapped the other hand in the fabric of her blouse and pulled on it. With a tearing sound, it gave and the front came away in his hand. The remainder of it fell, leaving her naked to the waist, and both men caught their breaths.

"Jesus . . ." Linc said. He released her wrist and pushed her back so that he could get a better look at her. "Jesus Christ . . ."

"I ain't never seen a woman so pretty," the other man said huskily.

She stood facing them, penned in by the counter, her breasts heaving as panic made her breathe faster. Their eyes roamed over her olive skin, the dark nipples . . .

"I wanna see the rest," the man behind Linc said anxiously.

"So do I," Linc said.

He moved toward her and she swung her hand to strike him, but he caught her wrist again. Holding her, he reached for her skirt and tore it off. It was made of better fabric than the blouse and did not come away as easily, but finally it tore and came away. He dropped it to the floor and backed away from her to drink her in.

"Look at that," he said.

She was fully naked now and their eyes lingered on the dark hair between her legs, her flaring hips, and her firm thighs and legs.

The man behind Linc moved forward as if to push past his friend, but Linc held his ground.

"Where are you going?" Linc demanded.

"I want her," the man said, glassy-eyed.

"Oh, no," Linc said, pushing the man back. "I unwrapped this package; I go first. Find a place where we can lay her down."

The man, staring at Delores, nodded eagerly.

"Go ahead!" Linc snapped.

On the second man's left was the entrance to the storeroom. He pushed aside the curtain and peered in and his eyes caught the stack of flour bags.

"In here," he said.

Delores' hand reached up onto a shelf and pulled down a leather quirt, a riding whip with a leather handle and a rawhide lash. As Linc turned back to her, she swung the quirt, the rawhide catching him across the left side of the face.

"Damn!" he cried out, rearing back and pressing his hand to his face. The lash had cut him, drawing blood, and he took his hand away and examined the bright redness that stained it.

"Hah," the other man said, laughing, "she gave it to you, boy!"

"Not yet," Linc said menacingly, "not yet she hasn't—but she will!"

When they finished with her, they left her lying sprawled across the flour sacks, crying. They had taken her, and then they had forced her to use her mouth, warning her that if she bit one of them, the other would kill her.

Now she lay there, weak and ashamed, afraid of what Dan would think when he came back. Would he still want her after the way she had been defiled by these animals?

Suddenly, she didn't want them to get away. If they got out the door, they'd never be caught, never be punished. The gun was still on the floor behind the counter.

She staggered down from the mound of sacks and stumbled to the doorway, still naked and still crying, but quietly now, lest she warn them. Her right breast hurt and was bleeding where one of them had bitten her, but she ignored the pain. As quickly as she could, she slipped through the curtained doorway and into the store where the two men were helping themselves to supplies, laughing, and filling up two empty flour sacks.

"Wasn't she something?" Linc asked.

"A real hellcat!"

"Whoowee, you said it."

Crouching down, she sneaked behind the counter on all fours and found the gun on the floor. It was a big, single-action Colt and would require both hands and all her strength to fire.

The two men moved toward the door now, preparing to leave, and this would be her only chance. She got up on her feet, leaned her elbows on the counter, and, using the thumbs of both hands, cocked the gun.

"Hey, I forgot—" the second man said, turning. When he saw her, he shouted for Linc to look out. Linc turned, reaching for his gun. As he drew, Delores fired. The bullet hit the other man in the left shoulder and he cried out in pain. Linc pointed his gun at Delores before she could cock her gun again. He fired, his bullet punching her between the breasts and knocking her back against the shelves. She struck with such force that one of the shelves came loose and fell, dropping everything it had been holding on top of her, driving her to the floor.

It seemed to her that she was falling in slow motion, but what truly surprised her was that there was no pain from the bullet. Her breast still hurt from the bite, but there was no pain from being shot.

That was curious, wasn't it?

TWO

Dan Rondo felt numb. He had felt that way since the sheriff told him about Delores.

Rondo had ridden into town and had become instantly aware that something was wrong. The people on the streets stared at him, eyes wide, and he knew damn well that something wasn't right.

Instead of directing his wagon to the livery stable, as he normally would have done, he kept going until he pulled to a stop in front of the store.

"Delores!" he shouted, jumping down.

He started for the door but a voice called out from behind him, stopping him.

"Dan."

He turned and saw the town sheriff, Lawson, crossing the street toward him. He never had much use for the man, but he stopped and waited for him.

"She's not inside, Dan."

"Where is she, Lawson?"

The tall, slender sheriff swallowed before speaking. "Rondo," he said, "she's . . . at the undertaker."

Rondo's eyes narrowed and he asked, "What happened?"

"Two men rode into town and went into the store. They were in there for a while, and as they were coming out there were some shots."

"Go on."

"They came running out. One of them was shot in the shoulder; the other one was bleeding from the face."

"And Delores?"

"When I went inside, she was on the floor behind the counter, Dan," the lawman said. "She was—didn't have clothes on. She was dead. Shot in the—the chest."

"Raped?"

Lawson nodded his head and stared at Rondo. Dan hadn't reacted the way he'd have thought. He was just standing there, staring at him with those cold eyes of his.

"Dan—"

"I want to see her."

"Sure, Rondo, sure."

They both walked to the undertaker's office in silence. Once there, the man, McCabe, took them into the back room where he had Delores Rondo laid out naked on a table.

Rondo turned and looked at the undertaker and then suddenly backhanded him across the mouth. McCabe, a large, fleshy man, hit the floor with a bang that shook the building, and he stared up at Rondo.

"Cover her up," Rondo said in a low, even tone.

The sheriff was still staring at Rondo, wondering when the wailing and screaming would start—but it wouldn't, he could now tell. This man wasn't the type—in fact, that was all he knew about this man, he realized.

Rondo walked to stand by his wife, while McCabe climbed to his feet and got something to cover her with. She was bruised and bloody, yet even in death she was so beautiful. He put his hand on her belly, where their child was. She had told him only last week that she was pregnant. She couldn't have been more than two months along. Now, they'd never see that baby—a son, she'd hoped—and he'd never hear her laugh or see her smile again.

"Rondo—" the sheriff said, moving next to him.

McCabe approached and covered Delores Rondo to the neck with a sheet. Dan Rondo took hold of the sheet and pulled it up the rest of the way, covering her completely.

"Rondo—" Lawson said again.

"No," Rondo said.

"No what?" Lawson asked.

"My name's not Rondo."

"Not Rondo?" the sheriff repeated. "I don't know what—"

"My name is not Rondo, sheriff," the other man said. "Dan Rondo is dead."

Lawson, afraid that the death of his wife had driven the man mad, said, "Uh, if you're not Dan Rondo, then who are you?"

"The name is Diamond," the man replied, "Ron Diamond."

And in that moment the Diamond Gun came back—with a vengeance.

THREE

Clint Adams' taste in women was, to say the least, wide-ranging. Pressed to indicate a preference, he would say that he liked a full-bodied and experienced woman, but the truth of the matter was that he simply liked women—all women—with only the most natural aversions to the too young, the too old, and the truly ugly.

Kendall Drake was full-bodied—though not in the way most men would prefer. She was full-breasted, but she did not possess the trim waist that society said desirable should have. To be polite, you would call her chunky, but when Clint saw her at the livery stable, he looked at her with admiration. She was wearing a man's work shirt and jeans that fit her tightly. She had strong thighs and a full behind, and he could see the muscles move in her legs as she walked out to greet him.

"Hello," he said.

"Howdy," she said, squinting at him, and he thought back to a chance encounter he'd had years ago with another girl who worked in a livery, that one a full-bodied girl who was missing one front tooth. This one, however, was even fuller of breast and thigh than that one had been, although she, too, had golden hair that hung past her shoulders.

He stared at her with frank admiration, a big, comfortable girl who, after his two weeks on the trail with only short stops here and there, stirred something inside of him. Maybe later . . .

"I'd like to put up my rig and team for the night."

"One night."

"So far," he said, "unless I find some reason to stay for another."

"Better get down, then, so I can get to it."

He climbed down from the rig and got a closer look at her. She appeared to be in her early twenties and was pleasant looking, if not pretty.

"And my horse," he added.

"Your horse."

He beckoned to her and took her around back where Duke was standing.

"Well, Jesus," she said, and it was she who stared in frank admiration now—at Duke. "What a monster. What an absolutely beautiful monster."

"Well, old Duke has been called a lot of things before . . ."

"Never beautiful?"

"Never a monster. Will you take good care of him?"

"You bet I will, mister."

"Clint," he said, "the name is Clint."

That was when she told him that her name was Kendall Drake.

"Pleased to meet you, Miss Drake. I feel that I'm leaving Duke in good hands."

"You sure are, Clint. Best damn hands in the county."

She held them up to show him and he recognized the power that she must have had in her hands from the constant handling of horses.

"I can see that, Kendall. Can you tell me where the nearest hotel is?"

"Town has but one," she said and gave him directions. "Can't get lost in a town this size."

"I guess not," he said, grabbing his saddlebags and rifle. "I'll be back a little later to see how Duke is doing. All right?"

"Come back anytime," she said, and her expression was completely guileless so that he was sure there was no hidden meaning in her words.

Well, almost sure.

The town was indeed small—one main street with a hotel, a saloon, and a sheriff's office and only a couple of side streets. If it weren't for Kendall, there would have been nothing that he could see to keep him in Flint, Colorado.

As he passed a small general store, he saw two horses tied out front, each with a sack hanging from the saddle, and as he continued on, he saw two men ascending a side stairway, one supporting the other, as if one were injured. There was a sign on the general store wall that told him the stairs led to the office of a Dr. Hart. More than likely one man was some cowboy or drifter helping his injured partner.

After Clint had passed them on his way to the hotel, the two men ascending the stairs to the doctor's office banged impatiently on the doctor's door.

"We should have stopped long before this," Sam Henderson complained to Linc Gilmartin. "I could have bled to death by now."

"Stop complaining," Linc snapped. "I told you we had to get as far away from that town as we could before we stopped for a doctor. Besides, it ain't all that bad."

"Sure, that's what you say," Henderson said. "You ain't the one with a slug in your shoulder."

"And if it wasn't for me, you might have another somewhere else," Linc said. "Now, just shut up and let me do the talking."

The door opened and a tall, sandy-haired man in his late forties appeared.

"Can I help you?"

"Inside," Linc said, putting his hand against the doctor's chest and pushing him into the room.

"Hey!" the doctor complained as Linc helped Henderson inside and then closed the door.

"My friend's got a bullet in his shoulder, Doc," Linc said, "and you're gonna take it out."

"You didn't have to push me," the doctor complained.

"If you don't get to it, I'll do worse than push you."

The doctor, a pragmatic man if nothing else, decided to shut his mouth and get the bullet out. "Lay your friend down on that table," he said. "I'll wash my hands." Hart washed up and went to the table.

Linc watched the man closely as he probed for the bullet, found it, and extracted it, while Sam Henderson cursed and complained.

"How did this happen?" the doctor asked, holding the bullet aloft a moment before dropping it into a porcelain bowl.

"That's none of your affair, Doc," Linc said. "Just get him bandaged up. We've got to get going."

"What about your face?" the doctor asked. "That's a wicked slash."

Linc ignored the doctor and said to Henderson, "Keep an eye on this guy while I take the horses to the livery for a while."

The doctor said, "You can't leave this man here."

Henderson's gun came out and he cocked it, showing the doctor the barrel.

"Just relax, Doc."

FOUR

The hotel was a small wooden structure that Clint wouldn't have trusted to stand up to a brisk wind. As he entered, he formed a similar opinion about the elderly clerk behind the desk.

"How long will you be staying?" the man asked him. He could swear that the top of the man's thinning head of hair was covered with a fine sheen of dust.

"One night," he said.

The man nodded, as if he were used to people coming in and staying for one night. Clint registered, accepted his key, and went to his room. He didn't ask about a bath because he wouldn't have trusted the water to be clean. He made do with the small amount of tepid water he found in the pitcher in his room. He stripped to the waist and used it to wash away as much of the trail dust as he could.

He dried off while standing at the window and saw one of the two men he'd seen earlier, apparently walking his and his partner's horse to the livery. From where he stood, he thought he could see an angry red welt across the side of the man's face. His friend must have been getting treatment for whatever his injury or illness was. He wondered if this town had ever seen three strangers at the same time before.

Clint put on a fresh shirt and left the hotel for the town's only saloon. There were two or three customers, the bored bartender, and an even more bored saloon girl.

"Beer," he said, and the bartender nodded and served him a warm beer.

"Can't get that any colder?" Clint asked after a sip and a grimace.

"Nope."

"Let me have a shot of whiskey," Clint said, pushing the beer away.

"You'll have to pay for the beer."

Clint flipped a coin onto the bar and said, "Give me the whiskey."

As the bartender poured the whiskey, the saloon girl sidled up alongside him and bumped Clint's thigh with her bony hip.

"Looking for some company, mister?"

He looked down at her and thought she was was fairly young and pretty in a way. She'd probably look pretty good to anyone just off the trail, and if he hadn't already seen Kendall, she might have appealed to him—though not enough to pay for her.

"No thanks," he said, picking up the shot, "just the whiskey."

He tossed it off and the cheap liquor burned its way down his throat.

"You don't know what you're missing," the girl said, licking her thin lips.

"I'll chance it," he said. "Thanks."

He left the saloon and, for want of somewhere else to go, went back to the hotel. If his team hadn't needed the rest, he might have left, but then there was Kendall, who was the only attractive thing he'd seen about this town so far.

In his room he sat down on the rickety bed for a moment. The next thing he knew he was lying on his back on the bed, waking up. A check of his watch showed that he'd had an hour's nap, and now he had awakened hungry.

Dare he try a meal in this town?

In his wagon he still had some provisions that he could eat. He decided to go back to the livery, check on Duke, and then ask Kendall if there was a safe place to eat. If not, he'd use his own supplies.

Linc did not return to the doctor's office for some time, and when he finally did, he found the doctor sitting stiffly in a straight-back chair, while Sam Henderson, still on the table, kept a wary eye on him.

"Well, where the hell have you been?"

"I had some errands to run, and I brought you this," he said, showing Henderson a bottle of whiskey.

"Well, give it here," Henderson said, reaching for it eagerly.

Linc didn't bother telling his partner that he'd stopped in the saloon for a while and stayed to talk with the lone saloon girl there. She wasn't much, especially when you compared her to the dark-haired gal in Canaan, but a woman was a woman.

As Henderson pulled the top off the bottle and took a healthy swallow, the doctor said, "What do you men intend to do with me?"

"We'll keep you company for a little while, Doc," Linc said, "just long enough for our horses to take a rest."

"And then?"

"And then we'll be on our way."

"I'd strongly advise you to give this man some rest before you start riding," the doctor said.

"We ain't got time for that," Linc said.

"Well, if you put this man on a horse now, he's going to bleed to death."

"Linc . . ." Henderson said, looking concerned.

"All right," Linc said, "one night. We'll stay one night."

At least he'd be able to go back to the saloon and use the whore.

"The hotel—"

"No hotel, Doc," Linc said. "We'll stay right here with you."

"You can't—"

"You gonna stop us?"

The doctor did not reply.

"You lie back and get some rest like the doc said," Linc told Henderson. "I'll be back later."

"Where you going now?"

"I've got to get something to eat and I'll bring you something to eat. You are hungry, aren't you?"

"Damn right, I am," Henderson said. "I'm starving. What about him?"

"Him?" Linc said, looking at the doctor. "Why, you won't be no trouble at all, will you, Doc?"

By the time Clint got to the livery, Duke's coat was glistening.

"I told you I'd take good care of him," Kendall declared proudly.

"So you did," Clint said, putting his hand on Duke's rump. "He didn't give you any trouble, did he? Sometimes he can get ornery with people."

"He was a perfect gentleman," she assured him. "I've always been able to get along with horses."

"And men?"

She regarded him for a moment and then said, "Some men, some time."

He looked around and saw the horses that belonged to the other two strangers.

"Population must have doubled today."

"Close to it," she said. "Why'd you pick this town to stop at?"

He shrugged and said, "It was next, and I had slept in my wagon the past three nights. Then again, that hotel room isn't much better."

"I sleep here," she said, "on the hay. Makes a real comfortable bed."

"You run this place alone?"

She nodded, idly running a brush over Duke's coat.

"It was my father's, but he's been dead for a couple of years."

"Must be lonely," he said, the remark coming from his lips innocently.

"Sometime."

"I was wondering if you'd be able to tell me where I could get something to eat?"

She made a face and said, "There's no really good place in town."

"Well, where do you eat?"

"I cook out back," she said and then looked at him and said, "I'll cook you something, if you like."

"Oh, I couldn't ask—"

"It wouldn't be any trouble," she said, cutting him off. "What you said about it being lonely here is true. I'd be obliged for somebody to talk to."

"All right, Kendall," he said, "that'd be fine."

She grinned happily, transforming her face from pleasant to genuinely pretty.

"I'll get right to it."

FIVE

Dinner was simple fare prepared on a wood-burning stove in a back room of the livery, where Kendall Drake apparently lived. There was a small pallet for sleeping—although, as she had previously explained, she preferred to sleep on the hay in the stable—a small wooden table at which they were seated, and the stove, used for cooking and for heat.

The conversation was enjoyable because they talked about what Kendall knew best, horses, and Clint was quite impressed by her obvious knowledge.

"Seems to me you could put your talent for handling horses to better use elsewhere," he commented.

She smiled sadly and said, "The trick is to get somewhere else. I'm saving my money, but it's slow in a place like this."

"I guess it would be," Clint said.

"Would you like more soup?" she asked.

"I've had enough, thanks," he said, handing her his bowl and utensils. "It was delicious, Kendall."

Shyly, she said, "Thanks, but it wasn't much."

She rose and excused herself for a moment, exiting through a back door to clean their utensils outside. She returned a moment later, and at that moment they heard a man's voice from inside the stable.

"Hey!"

She looked out the door that led from the room to the stable and said, "One of the strangers. I'd better see what he wants."

She left the room and Clint stood up and moved to the door so he could watch.

The man was the same one he had seen leading two horses to the livery earlier. Up close, he could see that the man was in his early thirties, but even if he hadn't had that angry cut across his face, he wouldn't have been anything but unpleasant looking. The wound across his face looked as if it had been inflicted with a whip.

"Can I help you?" she asked.

"Yeah," the man said, "we'll be leaving our horses overnight, after all."

"That's fine."

"For you, maybe," he said sourly. "We're gonna have to leave at daybreak, and I'll want the horses saddled and ready."

"If you want your horses saddled and ready at daybreak, you'll have to come and do it yourself," she explained. "I'll leave the door unlocked for you. You'll have to pay me now, though."

"For what?" he demanded. "For saddling our horses ourselves?"

"Mister, I feed your horse and I put him up. That's all you get. If you don't like it," Kendall said, "you can go to another stable."

"There ain't another livery in this poor excuse for a town."

"That's right."

"Why, you bitch—" the man said, moving toward her angrily. Clint had to give the young woman credit, for she didn't back up a step. He stepped out of the back room and into clear sight. The man stopped short as he spotted him.

"You'd better pay the lady," Clint said, "or take your horses elsewhere."

The man considered the situation for a moment, then dug into his jeans for money, and handed it to Kendall.

"Thanks," she said.

The man ignored her and looked at Clint.

"I'll see you again, mister."

Clint merely shrugged indifferently and the man turned and stalked out.

Kendall turned to Clint and said, "Thanks, but I could have handled him."

"I know you could have," Clint said, "but I was here and I wanted to help."

"Well," she said, "thanks, again."

She was in the act of moving past him to enter the back room when she impulsively kissed him on the cheek. Immediately she became embarrassed.

"I'm sorry."

"For what?" he asked. "It was very nice. Thank you."

He entered the room behind her and watched as she dropped the money into a coffee tin, which was apparently her bank.

"Well, I guess I'd better get to the hotel," he said. "I've got to get an early start in the morning."

"You won't be comfortable there," she said simply.

"Do you have another suggestion?"

"Yes," she said boldly, "you can stay here. I can fix you a hay bed. You'll be comfortable, and it won't cost you anything."

"I'll tell you what," Clint said. "I'll take you up on your offer, but I'll pay you as if this were a hotel."

"You don't have to—"

"Let's just call it my donation to your moving fund. If you

don't take it, I'll just sleep at the hotel.''

"All right," she said.

"I'll go and get my gear."

"I'll have your bed ready when you get back."

During the walk to and from the hotel, Clint fantasized about what he might find when he returned to the livery. He felt a stab of disappointment as he entered and saw that Kendall was still fully dressed.

"Your bed is in there," she said, indicating a stall where she had fashioned a hay mattress and covered it with a blanket.

"The blanket is clean," she assured him.

"Where are you sleeping?" he asked.

"Mine's over there," she said, pointing to a stall across the way and a little farther down from him. "It's where I always sleep."

"As long as I'm not taking your bed," he said, and she assured him that he was not.

"Well," she said then, "good night."

"Good night, Kendall."

She hesitated a moment, then moved down to her stall, and doused her lamp. He could hear the hay rustling as she laid down. He stripped down to his longjohns, extinguished the lamp she'd set up for him, and tried out the hay mattress. She was right; it was comfortable. It would have been more comfortable if she had been in there with him, but he resigned himself to a night alone and settled down to sleep.

Sometime later he woke and heard movement in the darkness. His gun was inches from his hand, but he didn't need it. A figure moved into the stall with him. It was Kendall. Warm and naked, she joined him on his hay bed. She brought several odors with her; her own muskiness and a touch of fear.

"Kendall . . ."

"I'd never forgive myself, Clint," she whispered, "if I didn't offer myself to you before you left in the morning. I'd never know if you wanted me or not. If you don't, I'll go back—"

He placed the index finger of his right hand against her lips and said, "I want you."

He kissed her mouth gently and palmed her big breasts. Her kiss was tentative, and he slipped his tongue into her mouth, causing her to react as if she'd been struck by lightning. He unbuttoned his longjohns until his penis was exposed, standing out long and hard, and he took her hand and placed it on him. Eagerly she took hold of him, but did not seem to know quite what to do next.

"I haven't been—I mean, I don't have much experience—" she stammered.

"Relax, Kendall," he said, his mouth working on her large nipples, worrying them between his lips, "just relax . . . Leave it to me."

He took a moment to remove his longjohns and then went back to her, molding his body to hers. His hands roamed her body, encountering what seemed to be acres of smooth, warm flesh. His fingers searched and, then finding, probed until she was wet and panting . . . and ready . . .

In a room over the saloon, Linc Gilmartin was in bed with the town whore who—if she weren't as pretty as the gal in Canaan—had been much more cooperative.

Now Linc sat up in bed and began to dress because he remembered that he had promised to bring Sam Henderson something to eat.

He thought about the big blond bitch in the livery—what a cushiony body that one had—and the man with her and wished that he could have killed both of them, but it wouldn't have been a smart move. Besides, he had a feeling he'd be seeing that dude again.

And then there was the fact that he already had a doctor to kill before he left town. It was a good idea to keep your killings to a minimum.

In the morning Linc nudged Henderson awake and said, "It's time for us to get a move on."

"Oooh," Henderson moaned, rising to a seated position. Sleeping on the examination table all night hadn't done much good for his shoulder. "I can't, Linc. I'm—I'm too damned sore to ride a horse."

"You too sore to swing from a tree by a rope?" Linc asked.

Henderson frowned and said, "All right, damn it, I'm getting up."

Hampered by his bad shoulder, he needed a few tries to get his gunbelt on, and by the time he did, Linc was waiting impatiently at the door.

"What about the doc?" Henderson said. "We can't just leave him here—"

"I took care of that while you were asleep, Sam," Linc said. "Come on; let's get moving."

Henderson looked over at the chair where Linc had tied the doctor up. The man was still seated there, still tied up, but there was a gaping wound in his throat, and his chest was covered with blood.

Linc Gilmartin had slit the doctor's throat without waking Henderson, and that made Sam Henderson shiver because he realized that Linc could have cut his throat just as easily.

Early in the morning Clint and Kendall made love again, slowly, enjoying each other as if it were the last time— which, of course, it was.

By the time the stranger came for his horses, they were in the back room, dressed and waiting for the coffee to be ready. They watched as the man saddled the two animals, muttering to himself, and then led them from the stable.

"Not a very friendly man," Clint said.

"That mark on his face . . ."

"His partner was apparently hurt more seriously than he was," Clint said, explaining when and how he had first spotted the two men.

"Well, I'm glad he's gone," she said. She moved to the stove and said, "The coffee's almost ready."

She said it sadly because he had told her that, after a cup of coffee together, he'd have to leave. As it turned out, after the coffee they went back to the hay bed for a little while more before Clint finally left.

He wondered what she'd say when she found the fifty dollars he'd left in her coffee tin.

When Clint left Flint, Colorado, there were a few things he was unaware of.

Number one was that he was going in the opposite direction from that taken by Linc Gilmartin and Sam Henderson.

Another thing was that Ron Diamond was traveling toward Flint, Colorado, hoping to catch up with the men who had raped and killed his wife.

The third thing he didn't know was that all three paths would eventually converge, and when they did, at least one person was going to die.

If he had known, he might have gone in a different direction. Maybe.

Ron Diamond, on the other hand, knew exactly what his path was leading him to—death . . . and he couldn't wait to get there.

SIX

Clint was camped for the night with a fire going and a pot of coffee and bacon and beans cooking. He was halfway between Flint, Colorado, and Canaan, New Mexico, and he was wondering if he should stop in Canaan to see how Ron Diamond—that is, Dan Rondo—and his wife were doing. He'd just decided against it when he heard a noise from the darkness around his camp.

He stood up, prepared to produce his gun at a second's notice, and listened intently.

"Hello the fire!" a voice called out.

"Come ahead," Clint called back, "slow and easy."

He heard the sound of a horse. A man appeared at the edge of the darkness and moved into the circle of light given off by the campfire. He was leading a horse. He recognized the man immediately.

It was Dan Rondo.

"Dan?"

Diamond approached and Clint saw the coldness of his face, the haunted look in his eyes.

"Not Dan," the man said as he reached Clint, "it's Ron Diamond."

"Diamond?" Clint said, frowning. "What happened?"

"Give me a cup of coffee and I'll tell you all about it," Diamond said. "I left Canaan without any supplies."

33

"Take care of your horse. I'll not only give you coffee; I'll feed you, too."

"Good enough."

By the time Diamond returned to the fire, Clint had the food divided up, half and half. Luckily, he'd made plenty.

"Why would you leave town without supplies?"

"I was in a hurry."

Clint wanted to ask why, wanted to ask about Delores, and he wanted to ask why Dan Rondo had become Ron Diamond again, but he knew he had to let the man get to it on his own.

Finally Diamond said, "All right, you deserve an explanation," and he told Clint what had happened in Canaan.

"Jesus, Ron," Clint said helplessly, "I'm sorry."

"I'm hunting them now," Diamond said. "That's why I left town without gathering supplies. I walked out of the undertaker's, saddled my horse, and rode out."

Clint asked, "What about the burial?"

"The undertaker will handle it," Diamond said. "I didn't want to let them get too far ahead of me."

"I can't blame you for that."

"Thanks."

"Do you have any idea what the men look like?"

"No, but I'll know them when I find them."

"How?"

"She shot one of them," Diamond said, "and I suspect she caught the other one across the face with a quirt. There was blood on a quirt and someone said one was riding out of town slumped on his horse."

"What?" Clint asked in surprise.

Diamond stopped eating immediately and stared at Clint.

"Does that mean something to you?"

"It sure does," Clint said, and he explained about his stopover in Flint.

"You saw them, then?" Diamond said. "You know their names?"

"Yes," Clint said, "but I don't know their names."

"But you can identify them."

"Yes."

"You've got to come with me, Clint," Diamond said. "You've got to help me."

"I'll go to Flint with you, Ron," Clint said, "but after that you're on your own." It sounded harsh, but he didn't want to get involved in someone else's thirst for revenge.

"But you know them! You can point them out!"

"Look, they were both going to the doctor in Flint," Clint said. "We'll go back there and talk to him. He should be able to tell you their names and then you won't need me."

Diamond stared at the Gunsmith until Clint said, "Your food's getting cold."

"All right," Diamond said. "I'll settle for that."

"Fine. Let's finish eating and turn in. We'll get an early start."

As they bedded down, Clint realized that once he had told Diamond about the doctor he had given himself a way out. Diamond didn't need him to show him where Flint was, so why had he agreed—offered, in fact—to go back with him?

Maybe it was to see Kendall again?

Well, that was as good a lie as any.

When they rode into Flint, Clint led Diamond right to the doctor's office. Diamond dismounted and Clint jumped down from the seat of his rig. Together, they mounted the stairs, Diamond in the lead, and when he reached the door, he kicked it in without hesitation.

"Ron," Clint said, rushing in after him, "take it easy—"

He pulled up short because he almost ran into Diamond's back. They both stared in shock at the man tied to the chair.

He was covered with his own blood and there was a gaping
wound in his throat.

"Is that the doctor?" Diamond asked.

"I never saw the doctor," Clint said, "but I'd say it was a
good bet."

"Shit!" Diamond cursed.

"We'd better see if there's some law in this town."

There wasn't, not officially, because Flint was barely a
town, but there was a man who acted in that capacity. His
name was Fellows, and he identified the dead man as the
doctor.

"I'll have him taken out," Fellows said. "You fellas
know who killed him?"

"We don't know any names," Clint said, "but we have an
idea."

"You after them?"

"Yes," Diamond said.

"Guess there ain't nothing for us to do but bury the doc,
then," Fellows said.

"You do that," Diamond said and left the office.

"Did he know the doc?" Fellows asked.

"No," Clint said, "neither one of us knew him at all."

"What's his problem, then?"

"It's personal," Clint said and left to go after Diamond,
whom he found waiting for him at the bottom of the stairs.

"I'm leaving, Adams," Diamond said, "and you're coming with me. You're the only one who can recognize one of
the killers."

"Let me tell you something, Diamond," Clint said.
"You're right. I am going with you, but not because you
asked me so nicely. I'm going because I liked your wife—
because I don't know enough to mind my own business—but
when this is done, you damn well better thank me."

"Clint—"

"You can either wait here or at the saloon," Clint cut in, "while I take care of having my rig and team put up."

"I'll meet you at the saloon."

"Fine," Clint said. "Give me a half hour."

Clint took his rig to the livery. Kendall was glad to see him. He explained his situation and asked her if she'd watch out for his rig and team while he was gone.

"Well, of course," she said. "This way I know you'll be back."

"You're right about that," he said, grinning at her.

She approached him and put her hands on his shoulders.

"I don't suppose you'd have time—"

"I wish I did, honey," he said, putting his hands on her waist, "but I've got to go. When I get back, we'll have plenty of time."

"I'm gonna hold you to that," she said, kissing him. "I'll saddle Duke for you."

While she saddled the big gelding, Clint took some supplies from his wagon. He settled for a hug and a kiss and he rode Duke to the saloon. Diamond was standing at the bar.

"Beer's warm," Diamond said.

"And the whiskey's poor," Clint said. "Are we gonna go or what?"

Diamond put his mug down with a loud bang and said, "Let's ride."

SEVEN

The only thing they had to go on was that the two men would certainly be riding away from New Mexico, which meant that they would have left Flint going in a northerly direction. They decided to ride north until they came to a town where they could ask if the two men had been through. If so, they would keep riding north. If not, they'd have to retrace their steps and pick another direction.

A day's ride brought them to the town of Morton's Corner, which, although larger than Flint, would still be classified as a small town.

"They couldn't have ridden through here unnoticed," Diamond said.

"Let's put the horses up at the livery and ask."

"Why put them up? If they came through here, we can keep going and catch up."

"The horses need rest, Diamond," Clint said. "If you kill your animal, you'll never catch them."

Grudgingly, Diamond agreed.

"Look, I'll take the horses to the livery; you check around town," Clint suggested. "Between us we should find out something."

"All right."

Diamond dismounted and handed Clint the reins.

"I'll meet you at the saloon," Diamond said, and Clint nodded and started for the livery.

"They've been ridden hard," he told the liveryman. "Cool them off, rub them down, and make sure they're properly fed. We'll be riding out in the morning."

"Well, this one looks like he can take it," the man said, eyeing Duke, "but that one's about had it."

Studying Diamond's roan, Clint decided that the man was right; the horse was done in. He'd have to talk to Diamond about buying another one.

"Any other strangers ride through in the past couple of days?" he asked.

"Why do you ask?" Clint could see the glint in the man's eye, as if he thought he might have some information that was worth money.

"I'm interested."

"Would you be willing to pay for the right answer?"

"Mister," Clint said, "all I'm looking for is the right answer, but I've got a friend with me who wouldn't mind just beating it out of you instead of paying for it. Now, you can talk to me or to him. Which will it be?"

The liveryman was short and fortyish with thinning hair and a pot belly. The threat was good enough to pry his tongue loose.

"Two men, couple of days ago," he said.

"What did you notice about them?" Clint asked vaguely, not wanting to put any thoughts into the man's head.

"One of them moved funny, like he was hurt," the man said. "The other one had a mark across his face. Here," he said, indicating his left cheek.

"Which way did they go when they left?"

"North."

"Any idea where they were headed?"

"Nope," the man said, "just north."

"Thanks."

"Hey," the man called out as Clint turned to leave, "ain't that worth something?"

"Just take care of those horses," Clint said, "and I'll talk to my friend about it."

"Well, what did these fellas do?"

"They got my friend mad," Clint called over his shoulder.

Ron Diamond entered the saloon and went right to the bar. If the men had been here, they'd be in need of a drink, especially the one Delores had shot.

He was trying not to think of Delores too much—the way she felt in his arms, the way she smelled and tasted—because if he did he'd start to grieve, and he didn't have time for that—yet.

"Beer," he told the bartender, and when the man brought it, Diamond clamped his hand down on his wrist before he could leave.

"Something else?"

"Information."

"Sorry, fresh out," the bartender said. Diamond's grip was tight, but the bartender, a huge man with powerful forearms, was not intimidated. He pulled his arm free and started to walk away.

"I'm interested in whether or not two strangers were here in the last couple of days."

The bartender stopped, looked past him, and then looked at him. In the mirror Diamond saw the men he had peeked at, three of them seated at a table.

"Sorry, I can't help you," the bartender said.

"Can't or won't?"

"Whatever, mister."

As the bartender started to move away, Diamond grabbed

for his arm again, clamping his right hand around the man's wrist.

"You got a good grip, mister," the bartender said, "but if you don't take your hand away, I'm gonna break it."

Diamond cursed himself silently for using his gun hand to grab the man. Now, he'd have to back off, but he had no doubt that the man was capable of doing what he said.

"All right," Diamond said, releasing his hold, "but I still want some answers."

"Maybe we can help?" someone from behind him said, and Diamond thought that he really was getting old and that he was out of practice. Even with the mirror behind the bar, he'd been so involved with the bartender that he hadn't seen the three men come up behind him. He turned to face them now and saw Clint Adams enter through the doors.

When Clint entered the saloon, he saw Ron Diamond backed against the bar by three men. He was tempted to let Diamond fend for himself, but he knew that the man was out of practice as far as dealing with hard cases.

"You having a problem, Ron?" Clint asked, approaching the group at the bar. From the look on the bartender's face, Clint judged that he was involved as well.

It was the bartender who responded. "Is this fella a friend of yours?"

"Sorta."

"Well, you'd better get him out of here before he gets himself hurt."

"Why would he do that?"

"He's asking too many questions for his own good."

"Maybe he's looking for some answers."

"Well, he ain't gonna find them here," one of the three men said.

"What have you fellas got against answering questions?" Clint asked.

"We don't like it," the bartender said.

"Well, you don't have to like it," Clint said. "All you have to do is do it, and I'd advise you to do it fast."

"Boys—" the bartender said, but Clint didn't give the man a chance to issue any orders. He swung at the closest man, catching him on the jaw with his left. Diamond brought up a knee into one man's groin, dropping him to the floor, and then kicked him into unconsciousness. Clint stepped in and hit the third man in the stomach. As he bent over from the blow, Diamond hit him on the jaw, and he slumped to the floor with his two friends.

Clint and Diamond faced the bartender now and Clint said, "You ready to answer some questions?"

"Are you kidding?" the man said. "I'm just getting started with you two."

The huge man vaulted over the bar, causing Clint and Diamond to step back. Out from behind the bar, he looked even bigger.

"You ready?" Clint asked.

"Ready as I'll ever be."

Both men knew that they wouldn't use their guns against this man, who was unarmed, so they were going to have to try to subdue him without the weapons they were so proficient with.

They moved in on the man warily, but he moved fast for a big man, backhanding Ron Diamond so that he went flying across one table and then swinging his other hand and catching Clint across the face. The blow rocked his head back and knocked him onto the floor.

"Get up and ask your questions, fellas," the man invited. "Come on."

They got up and tried again. They attacked from either side, each grabbing one of the giant's legs in an attempt to upend him. He kicked one leg, sending Diamond to the floor, and then the other, doing the same to Clint.

"You fellas aren't doing too well."

Clint and Diamond looked at each other and Diamond said, "Maybe just one bullet?"

"Let's try again."

This time the big man caught them coming in. He pushed Diamond to the floor and then slammed his forearm across Clint's chest, stunning him. The man picked up Diamond, walked him to the door, and tossed him into the street. He went back to Clint, picked him up, and threw him out.

When Clint landed painfully on his back in the street, Diamond had already struggled to a seated position.

"That's it," Diamond said. "I'm gonna get some answers even if I have to use my gun."

"Don't bother," Clint said, pushing himself to a seated position and wincing at the pain it caused in his butt.

"What do you mean?" Diamond asked.

"They rode through here a couple of days ago," Clint said. "The liveryman said they rode out headed north."

"Was he sure it was them?"

"Described them perfectly."

Diamond stared at Clint and said, "Well, if you knew that, why'd we have to start a fight in there?"

"I didn't start the fight," Clint said. "You did."

"We could have walked out," Diamond said. "You could have told me that you already had the information."

Clint looked at the other man, shrugged, and said, "What can I say? You're right."

"Jesus," Diamond said, standing up slowly.

"Where are you going?"

"Inside," Diamond answered. "I need a drink."

"So do I," Clint said, struggling to his feet and following Diamond. "I sure hope we don't have to fight him for one."

EIGHT

As in Flint, there was only one hotel in town, but this one was considerably larger and offered more comfort. It even had a bathhouse, which both Clint and Diamond made use of.

Clint went to Diamond's room and suggested that they get something to eat.

"I'm not hungry," Diamond said.

"You'll get hungry."

"I've got some jerky in my saddlebags."

"Meet me at the saloon later for a drink?"

"I don't think so."

"Suit yourself," Clint said. "I'll pick up some supplies while I'm out. We can get started early in the morning."

"Fine. I'll be ready."

Clint hesitated outside Diamond's door, trying to think of something else to say, but then gave up and left. He heard Diamond shut the door gently behind him.

Clint had a completely unsatisfactory dinner in a café near the hotel—the coffee was atrocious. Then he went to the general store and purchased some supplies, which the owner promised to have ready by morning. After that, he went back to the saloon where he and Diamond had scuffled.

When they had picked themselves up off the street earlier

and gone into the saloon, the big bartender had said, "You coming back for more?"

"We're coming back for a drink," Clint had replied. "Do we have to fight for that, too?"

"Can you pay?"

"We can."

"Then come ahead and drink."

The bartender had vaulted the bar again and set up their drinks.

Now, as Clint entered again, the bartender saw him and waved him over. As Clint approached the bar, he looked around and saw that the place was very busy.

As he reached the bar, the man put up a beer and said, "On the house."

Clint frowned and asked frankly, "Why?"

"You're the Gunsmith, right?"

"Who told you that?"

"Somebody who was in before. Is it true?"

"Yes, it's true."

"And your friend?"

"His name is Ron Diamond."

"Diamond . . ." the man said, then recognition dawned, and he said, "The Diamond Gun? I thought he was dead!"

"Well, he's not."

"How do you like that?" the bartender said. "The Gunsmith and the Diamond Gun in my place."

"Does that make a difference?"

"It sure as hell does," the bartender said. "Either one of you could have killed me easily, but you both chose to fight fair. I gotta respect that."

"That's worth a beer, huh?"

"Sure is."

"What's your name?"

"Willie Banks."

"Well, Willie, how about some answers?" Clint asked, picking up the beer. "Is it worth some answers?"

"Well," the man said, rubbing his jaw, "as much as I hate answering questions, I guess it would be worth it. Go ahead; ask away."

Clint drank some beer first and then put the mug down. "Two men, one with a mark across his cheek and the other moving like he might have been hurt."

"The shoulder," the bartender said, "he had something wrong with his shoulder. I figured he'd taken a bullet there recently."

"He did," Clint said. "So you saw them?"

"Sure. They were in here for a drink and left the next day."

"What can you tell me about them?"

The man shrugged and said, "Nothing."

"Nothing at all? You didn't hear them talking?"

"Nope," the man said. "They took their drinks and sat at a table."

"Anybody sit with them that you could see?"

"No."

"Did they appear to know anyone in town?"

"No."

"They didn't, uh, play cards with anyone?"

"Nothing," the bartender said. "They had their drinks and then left. I guess to the hotel. They didn't talk to anyone but each other while they were here."

So the bartender really couldn't tell him anything that the liveryman hadn't. He simply verified that the two men had been in town.

Clint finished his beer and looked around the place. The three men he and Diamond had knocked out were not present, and of all the men who were, there were no more than two at any table and there didn't seem to be a chance for a poker game.

He put the empty beer mug down and said, "All right, thanks for the beer."

"My pleasure. Hey, I'm sorry about what happened before. I just get tired of people thinking that bartenders are just supposed to answer every question thrown at them. You know what I mean?"

"Sure," Clint said, "no hard feelings."

Clint left the saloon and, since his options were limited, decided to return to the hotel and turn in for the night. As he was turning in, he remembered that he wanted to talk to Diamond about getting a new horse. He walked down the hall and knocked on Diamond's door. When there was no answer, he knocked again and then tried the doorknob. Diamond had either turned in and forgotten to lock the door, or he'd left the room and left it open.

Clint pushed the door in gently and entered, wondering how Diamond's instincts were after all these years? Had he become that heavy a sleeper?

As he entered the room, he saw that this was not the case. Diamond had indeed left his room.

Had he suddenly become hungry or thirsty? Or perhaps, with the death of his wife being so recent, sleep did not come easily to him and he'd gone for a walk?

Should he go look for him? He decided not to. Ron Diamond was a big boy and didn't have to explain his actions to anyone.

He started to leave the room and then stopped short, struck by an odd urge to look through Diamond's saddlebags, which were lying on top of the bed. He thought a moment, and since he had no idea what he would have been looking for, he continued out of the room, down the hall, and into his own room.

During the night he thought he heard someone walk down the hall, but whether it was Diamond or not really didn't make a bit of difference.

The next morning Diamond was already at the livery when Clint arrived.

"You're up early," Clint said.

Diamond turned around at the sound of his voice and then turned back to the horse he was inspecting.

"I need a new horse."

"Yeah, I noticed that yesterday," Clint said. "Meant to tell you about it last night. I see I didn't have to."

"I guess not."

"I did knock on your door last night, but apparently you didn't hear me."

"You know that's not the case," Diamond said. "You were in my room last night; you know I wasn't there."

"I wasn't going to mention that. I didn't want you to feel as if you owed me an explanation."

"I don't," Diamond said, leaning over to study the horse's legs, "but I couldn't sleep and went for a walk."

"Fine," Clint said, accepting his short explanation.

At that point the liveryman entered and Diamond turned toward him.

"I'll take this one," he said, and both men went off to haggle out a price while Clint saddled Duke and, for Diamond he saddled the horse he planned to purchase.

When Diamond returned, he checked his saddle, tightened the cinch—an action from which Clint took no offense—and then mounted.

"We picking up some supplies?" he asked Clint.

Clint nodded. "At the general store."

"Let's get moving, then."

"After we get started," Clint said, "I'll tell you what the bartender told me last night."

Miles ahead, in a town called Largo, Linc Gilmartin and Sam Henderson were sitting in a saloon, having a drink and discussing the possibility of someone's following them.

"I don't think it's very likely at this point, Sam," Linc said. "We've come some distance, and that one-horse town wasn't likely to have much of a lawman, let alone enough men to put together a posse." He took a drink and, pouring himself another from the bottle, said, "I think we're in the clear."

"What about the husband?" Henderson asked, flexing his stiffening, wounded arm.

"What about him?" Linc asked. "What kind of a threat could a shopkeeper be against us?"

Henderson thought that over for a moment and then, pouring himself another drink, said, "Yeah, I guess you're right. Why should we worry about some shopkeeper?"

NINE

Clint Adams and Ron Diamond rode through the town of Largo and several towns after it, all of which had also been passed through by the two men they were seeking. In none of those towns, however, were they able to come up with a name.

Soon, they crossed from Colorado into Wyoming, where they met with similar results, until they came to a town called Duneden, where the trail suddenly came to a stop.

After putting up their horses, the two men split up, but met later in the Half Dollar Saloon.

"Anything?" Clint asked. Diamond had arrived first and now Clint, beer in hand, joined the Diamond Gun at the back table he had claimed.

"No, nothing," Diamond said.

"Talk to the bartender?"

"Yes."

"They must have changed direction between here and the last town, Hammond," Clint said. "But which way? The Dakotas? Idaho? Toward Utah? Are they covering their tracks?"

"I don't think so," Diamond said. "What do they have to fear? They've got to figure there's no posse or lawman after them, and why should they worry about some shopkeeper?

53

No, if they've changed direction, it's not meant as any kind of evasive action.''

''So then all we've got to do is go back and pick up their trail again.''

''What kind of a tracker are you?''

''So-so,'' Clint said. ''What about you?''

''I wasn't all that good years ago,'' Diamond admitted, ''so I'd be even worse now.''

''Well, if they're not covering their trail, we should be able to pick it up.''

''We still have a couple of hours of light.''

''The horses are tired, and who knows how far we'll have to go back before we find the point where they changed direction? I think we'd be better off waiting until morning, Ron.''

Diamond thought it over a few seconds and then nodded.

''As usual, you're right, Clint,'' he said. There had been no outward sign of anxiety or impatience on Ron Diamond's part, but obviously he had been holding it in check inside of himself.

''I guess we'd better get a couple of rooms,'' Clint said, standing up.

Diamond stood and they left the saloon together. When they reached the walk outside, they noticed a ruckus across the street.

''Look at that,'' Clint said.

Three boys were fighting with one, all of whom looked to be about ten or so, although the lone boy was somewhat smaller than the others. In spite of this, he seemed to be holding his own pretty well, but Clint knew that the weight of numbers would soon tell against him.

''Why don't you go ahead and get the rooms?'' Clint said to Diamond.

''You gonna play referee?''

"Peacemaker," Clint said, stepping down into the street. Diamond watched him for a moment, then shook his head, and headed for the hotel.

When Clint reached the boys, the three had taken the one to the ground by virtue of their superior weight. Clint took hold of two of the boys by the back of their belts and lifted them off, setting them gently aside, and then did the same with the third. The smaller boy then got to his feet and glared at the three boys and Clint Adams. Blood came from his nose.

"Come on, you cowards," he called to the others, "I can take you all!"

"The fight's over, boys," Clint said, positioning himself between the combatants.

"Get out of the way, mister!" the small boy shouted. "I can take them."

"I'm sure you can, son," Clint said, putting his hand on the eager and somewhat battered boy's shoulder, "but I don't want you to hurt them anymore."

"Ha, he didn't hurt us," the largest of the boys said contemptuously.

Clint looked at that boy and said, "Does three against seem fair odds to you, son?"

"He started it."

"I did not!" the small boy shouted.

"Maybe we should take you to your folks, son," Clint said to the small boy.

"He don't have no folks," the largest boy said. The remark was made with so much satisfaction that Clint now had no doubt as to who started the fight. The smaller boy was obviously an orphan who had taken as much teasing as he could and was fighting back the only way he knew how.

"Do you boys have folks?" Clint asked.

"Of course we do."

"Then you'd better get back to them."

The three boys sneered at the small boy, but turned and sauntered off, laughing and patting each other on the back.

"What's your name?" Clint asked the bloody-nosed boy. He was blond with light blue eyes and a pale complexion that probably didn't take kindly to the sun. He was a good-looking boy in spite of the blood that smeared his face.

"Todd."

"Well, Todd, suppose you tell me where you live?"

The boy hung his head and said, "At the orphanage outside of town."

They hadn't passed an orphanage entering town, so Clint assumed that it was probably north of town.

"Why don't I take you back there?"

"I can find my own way back."

"Well, I think when I show you my horse you'll want to ride back."

"Why?" the boy asked, curiosity aroused.

"You'll see," Clint said. "Let's walk to the livery."

Todd was properly impressed with Duke and watched, wide-eyed, while Clint saddled the giant gelding. That done, he lifted Todd into the saddle, then mounted behind him, and followed the boy's directions to the Duneden Home for Orphaned Children.

As they approached the building, a ramshackle, wooden house, several children came running toward them, shouting Todd's name. There were boys and girls of all ages, and they surrounded Duke as he continued on toward the house, being very careful—instinctively—not to trample any of the small children beneath his massive hooves.

Clint saw the front door of the house open. A few other children came running out and were followed by a woman who, from this distance, seemed full-bodied. She moved toward Clint, Duke, and Todd with a self-assured stride. As they moved closer to each other, he could see that she was in her early thirties and very attractive with honey-colored hair that she wore in a tight bun.

"That's Mrs. Sharpe," Todd said. "She runs the orphanage."

"Todd—" Mrs. Sharpe said, as Clint reined Duke in.

"Mrs. Sharpe, I'm Clint Adams," he said, introducing himself. He lowered Todd to the ground and said, "I found this boy fighting three others and stepped in before he could hurt them too seriously."

Todd puffed his chest out and Clint saw a smile tug at the woman's mouth before she gained control over it.

"I see," she said. "Todd, I've warned you about fighting before."

"Yes, ma'am."

"Now get yourself inside and cleaned up. Dinner is almost ready."

"Yes, ma'am." Todd turned to Clint and said, "See you, Clint. You too, Duke."

"Good-bye, Todd."

Todd ran into the house and Mrs. Sharpe shouted for all of the other children to follow. They obeyed her and in moments she was standing alone.

"My name is Nancy Sharpe, Mr. Adams," she said, peering up at him. "I want to thank you for what you did for Todd. He's always fighting."

"I suppose the others boys tease him," Clint said. "The ones who have folks, I mean."

"Yes, they do, constantly."

"Maybe if you had the children travel in pairs or groups at all times, the others would leave them be, Mrs. Sharpe. There's sometimes safety in numbers."

She regarded him for a moment with her head tilted very

attractively to one side and then said, "That makes a lot of sense, Mr. Adams. I'll talk to the children about that."

"You do that, Mrs. Sharpe," Clint said. "Good evening."

Clint started to turn Duke around for the trip back to town when Mrs. Sharpe called out to him, stopping him in mid-turn.

"Mr. Adams."

"Yes, Mrs. Sharpe?"

She smiled and asked, "Would you like to stay for dinner? We have plenty and I'm sure the children would be interested in talking to you."

"Why is that?"

"Well you are the man people call the Gunsmith, aren't you?"

Clint frowned unhappily and said, "I've been called that, yes."

"You don't sound happy about it."

"I'm not."

"That's perfect." When he frowned, she went on. "You see, many of the children—especially the boys—tend to idolize gunfighters."

"I see."

"I don't think you do," she said. "I was wondering if perhaps you would talk to them and tell them what that kind of life is really like. Perhaps you could show them the way to other heroes, rather than men who kill."

"Like me?"

"I didn't say that, Mr. Adams," she replied. "I have an open mind about these things. I will listen to you just as intently as the children will."

He thought it over a moment and then decided to accept this handsome woman's offer, just so she could learn how different from other gunfighters he truly was.

"Very well, Mrs. Sharpe," he said. "I accept your invitation."

"Wonderful," she said, clapping her hands together for a moment. "I'm afraid I don't have anyone to care for your horse, but there is a stable around back."

"I'll take care of him myself."

"Dinner will be ready by the time you come inside," she assured him. "Just follow your nose to find the dining room."

She turned to walk to the front door and he watched with pleasure as her behind moved interestingly. At the door she turned and caught him watching her.

"I hope that in the presence of the children you will continue to call me Mrs. Sharpe," she said, "but otherwise you may call me Nancy."

"I'd be honored," he said.

She flashed him a quick smile and then disappeared inside.

TEN

Dinner was an unusual situation for Clint Adams. He was introduced to the children as the infamous Gunsmith, and from that point on, the floor was opened to questions, of which there were many, delivered in rapid-fire fashion. Clint did his best to field them all and answer them honestly, for he felt that was all he had to do to show these children that the life of a so-called gunfighter was not one to be envied or romanticized. Throughout the meal, he saw Nancy Sharpe nodding and watching him approvingly, and for some reason this made him feel good.

Dinner was served by Mrs. Olson, the cook, who, Nancy told him, was the only other staff member. She was being assisted by a lovely red-haired girl who appeared to be in her late teens, and Clint questioned Nancy about her.

"I thought you said Mrs. Olson was the only other staff member?"

"Oh, that's Belinda," Nancy explained. "She was one of the children here, and after she turned eighteen, she asked if she could stay. She's a sort of unofficial staff member, working only for room and board. The other children love her, so she's a great help to me." At that moment, Belinda placed a plate of food before Clint and boldly stared at him for a moment before withdrawing. He noticed that she had beautiful green eyes.

"I think she's got her eye on you, Clint," Nancy said in a whisper. "Be careful. She's been precocious since she was sixteen."

Watching the shapely young girl walk back to the kitchen, Clint could think of other words to describe her.

When dinner was completed, the children set about cleaning the table and removing the utensils to the kitchen. Even the boys helped. All of the children in the orphanage were present at the meal. Clint counted twenty, eight girls and twelve boys, and they all helped.

Clint rose and Nancy Sharpe approached him.

"Would you like to go for a walk?" she asked him.

"The children—"

"Mrs. Olson will keep them busy," Nancy said. "I'd like very much to talk to you . . . alone."

Clint nodded and hoped that Ron Diamond wouldn't start to worry much about him.

In fact, Ron Diamond was not worried at all. He was seated in the saloon, working on a bottle, and was the object of some conversation at a table across the room. Three men were betting as to whether or not the stranger was the Diamond Gun, a man who was supposed to be dead.

Pretty soon, they'd work up the nerve to get up and find out.

Nancy Sharpe took Clint for a walk out behind the orphanage, through a stand of trees to a small pond. After a moment of silence, he took her in his arms and kissed her, thinking that this was what she wanted, that this was why she had asked him to stay and to walk. She responded for fleeting moments, her mouth going soft and pliant, but then she placed her hands against his chest and pushed away.

"This is not why I asked you to come for a walk, Clint."

"It's not?" he asked, releasing her. "Now, I am confused, Nancy."

"I'm sorry," she said, turning her back, "I didn't mean to
. . . to lead you on. I do like you and perhaps later . . . but
not now."

"What's wrong with now?"

"I have something to talk to you about," she said. Then
she turned to face him and added, "Something very, very
important."

"To who?"

"To me, I admit," she said, "but mostly to those children."

"All right," Clint said, folding his arms, "go ahead and
talk."

"I need your help," she said, "or I'll lose this place and
these children will be homeless."

"Tell me about it, Nancy."

They sat on the ground and she explained her problem to
him. She told him that the orphanage and the land it was on
lay between two ranches, and the owners of those ranches
were after the land.

"It's a bone of contention between them," she said, "and
it doesn't matter to them that the children need a place to
live."

"You don't intend to sell, do you?"

"I don't want to, but I may not have a choice. They might
force me to sell."

"How?"

"So far there have just been vague threats from both sides,
remarks made at me and the children when we go to town to
shop."

"Where does your money to run the school come from?"

"We were receiving money from back east. We're one of
many schools in the west that are supported by eastern funds,

but suddenly the money just stopped coming. We have some in the bank in town, but it's almost gone."

"Do you think one of the ranchers had something to do with the money not coming anymore?"

"That's all I can think of."

"What do you want me to do, Nancy?"

"They won't listen to me, Clint," she said, leaning forward and putting a hand on his knee, "but maybe they'd listen to you."

"Because I'm the Gunsmith?"

"Because you're a man," she said. "Will you help us?"

"I don't know what I can do," Clint said, "but I'll give it a try. I'll talk to them tomorrow."

He wondered how Diamond would react to this plan, but at the most it would only cost them the morning.

During the walk back to the house, Nancy gave Clint the names of the two ranchers and then invited him to spend the night at the orphanage.

"I can't," he said. "I have a friend in town who might be wondering where I am. I'll have to tell him my plans for tomorrow."

"Will he object?"

"If he does, he can go on without me."

When they reached the house, they stopped and she turned to face him.

"I don't know how to thank you."

"I haven't done anything yet, Nancy," he said, touching the smooth skin of her face. "Thank me if and when I do."

She hesitated a moment and then said, "I have to go back inside."

"I'll saddle my horse and be on my way."

"Will you come back tomorrow?"

"Right after I've spoken to both men, I'll let you know what happens."

"I'll see you tomorrow, then."

Again she hesitated, then impulsively kissed him on the cheek, and rushed into the house.

Clint went to the small stable behind the house to saddle Duke, but found someone waiting there for him.

"I knew you'd come here after talking with Nancy," Belinda said.

She was smiling at him and the effect was dazzling, but not as dazzling as the fact that she was naked, her dress lying on the ground at her feet. Her body was bursting with youthful womanhood; her breasts firm and small, tipped by rusty-colored nipples; her hips slim and almost boyish.

"Belinda," Clint said, "I don't think you should be here."

"Why not?" she asked. "I saw you watching me inside."

"You're very hard not to watch," he admitted.

"And I was watching you. So was Nancy. She likes you a lot, but she's too inhibited to do something like this. I'm not."

"I can see that."

"I fixed the hay, so we can use it," she said, indicating a small bed she had fashioned from the hay. Clint thought that he was meeting a lot of women lately who liked to do it on hay.

"I'd really love to stay awhile, Belinda, but I've got to get back to town."

"Really?" she asked. She moved closer to him and put her hand over his crotch, where she could feel him bulging. "Right away?"

She got so close that he could feel the heat coming from her body, and then her breasts were pressed against him, the nipples erect. Her nostrils were flaring as her breath came

faster and, with surprising speed and strength, she had pulled
his head down and kissed him avidly, her tongue alive in his
mouth.

She was certainly no virgin and knew exactly what she was
doing. As if they had a life of their own, his hands slid down
her bare back to cup her solid buttocks and pull her tightly
against him. She laughed deep in her throat and chewed his
lips gently, happily, feeling that for the first time in her young
life she was about to be had by a real man.

As for Clint, what was a man to do with a bundle of energy
like this that threw itself into a man's arms?

He lifted her in his arms and carried her to the hay bed she
had prepared. Her lips were moving over his neck as he stood
next to the bed of hay and suddenly opened his arms.

"Wha—" she began, but stopped short when she hit the
ground. "What are you doing?" she demanded, looking up
at him, both puzzled and angry.

"I have to get back to town, Belinda," he explained. He
moved to Duke, mounted, then looked down at her, and said,
"Maybe another time."

Just as he knew she was certainly no virgin, he realized that
she was very well acquainted with the words she was hurling
at him as he rode away—highly unladylike words!

ELEVEN

Ron Diamond had become aware that he was the object of some scrutiny. The part of Dan Rondo that was still alive in him told him to get up and leave, but the old Diamond Gun replied that he had every right to expect to be allowed to sit in a saloon and enjoy a drink.

Only other people didn't quite see it that way.

The three men who were studying him were Rick and Paul Tyler and Cleon James. It was James who fancied himself a gunman, and it was he who thought he recognized the stranger as the Diamond Gun.

"Still think it's him?" Paul Tyler asked.

"I'm dead sure."

"Maybe you'll just be dead if you try to prove it," Rick Tyler said.

"Not a chance," James said, shaking his head. "He's an old man."

James himself was twenty-five, and he knew that Ron Diamond had to be close to fifty. Still, it was always smart to hedge your bet.

"Look, you fellas back me, standing on either side of me, and we can take him."

"You're the gunman, Cleon," Paul Tyler said, exchanging a glance with his brother. "You take him alone."

"All right," James said, "if you fellas don't want your share of the glory—"

"What glory?" Paul asked.

"The men who killed the Diamond Gun?"

The Tyler boys looked at each other and admitted to themselves that it didn't sound bad.

"What about it?"

The brothers looked at the stranger who, in addition to being close to fifty years old, had drunk most of a bottle of whiskey.

"All right," Rick Tyler said, speaking also for his brother. "If you're sure you can take him . . ."

"I can take him," Cleon James said. "You fellas are just my insurance."

They all looked at each other, nodded, and rose.

Ron Diamond saw the three men stand up and knew that he should have listened to that small remnant of Dan Rondo that still survived inside him. By not doing so, he effectively snuffed out Dan Rondo forever.

What remained was the Diamond Gun.

Cleon James approached the stranger's table with a Tyler boy on either side. Upon closer inspection, he could see the lines around the Diamond's eyes and the gray in his hair, and he began to feel even more confident.

"Hey, you," James said, stopping in front of Ron Diamond's table.

The man looked up and said, "Are you talking to me?"

"That's right, old man," James said, "I'm talking to you. Ain't you the man called the Diamond Gun?"

"That's right."

"Hell, I thought you were dead."

"Well, as you can see, I'm not."

"You sure as hell did get old, though."

"If you want to do the same, son, I suggest you go back to your table."

"Hey, is that a threat?"

The older man caught the younger man's eyes, held them, and said, "That's just good advice, son, for you and your friends."

"What do you think, fellas?" James asked, looking at the Tylers. "You think that's good advice?"

"We're with you, Cleon," Rick Tyler said.

"They're with me," James said to Diamond.

"Cleon? Is that your name?" Diamond asked.

"That's right."

"Well, Cleon, my gun is already out and it's pointing at you from under the table. Now, if you want to try your luck, make your move."

"Cleon—" Paul Tyler said nervously.

"He's bluffing," Cleon James said. "You're bluffing, old man."

Diamond shrugged and remained silent. James saw that both of the man's hands were below the table, and his own hands started to sweat.

"If you had any guts, you'd holster it and face me like a man."

"All three of you? Is that your idea of being a man? Facing three men? I call that being dead. No, we'll do it this way, son, or we won't do it at all."

It was all up to Cleon James, now. Ron Diamond, Rick Tyler, and Paul Tyler were all waiting for him to make up his mind.

"You're bluffing," he finally said, his right hand streaking for his gun. There was an explosion and a bullet tore through the table and then tore through Cleon James before he could even touch his gun.

As the man fell to the floor, Diamond brought the gun out from underneath the table. Paul Tyler moved for his gun and Diamond snapped off a shot, catching the man in the shoulder. As he spun with the impact of the bullet and fell to the floor, Rick Tyler threw his hands up and cried out, "Not me!"

"That man looks like your brother," Diamond said.

"He is."

"Then get him out of here and count both of you lucky to be alive."

"Yes, sir," Rick Tyler said. He bent to help his brother to his feet and then, with a last glance at the body of Cleon James, assisted his brother out of the saloon.

The bartender came around as Diamond holstered his gun and said, "I guess he was asking for it."

"He was."

"If you're the Diamond Gun, though, couldn't you have taken him fair and square?"

Diamond peered up at the man and asked, "What's fair and square have to do with staying alive? You ever faced a young gunman?"

"No, but—"

"Well, until you have keep your opinions to yourself. You'd better see about getting that man out of here."

As the bartender began pointing out other customers to help with the body, the doors opened, and a man wearing a badge stepped in. He spotted Diamond and walked to his table.

"You Ron Diamond?"

"I am."

The lawman almost went for his gun and then thought better of it. Instead, he folded his arms across his chest and said very deliberately, "You're under arrest."

Diamond looked up at the sheriff and then at the whiskey bottle on the table, which had liquid enough in it for one more drink. He said, "Mind if I finish my bottle?"

TWELVE

It was dark when Clint returned to town. After he left Duke at the livery, he checked the hotel to see if Diamond had returned to his room. Finding that he hadn't, he decided to check the saloon.

He entered the Half Dollar Saloon and found it virtually empty. He started to leave and then decided to have one drink before turning in.

"A beer," he ordered.

"Pretty near closing," the bartender said.

"I'll drink it fast."

The man shrugged, drew the beer, and set it in front of Clint.

"I'm looking for a friend of mine and I thought I'd find him here."

"That him?" the bartender asked, pointing to a man who was sitting at a table with his head on it.

"No, that's not him."

"Then I guess he's not here."

"Maybe he was here earlier?"

"What's he look like?"

"His name is—"

"I don't find out my customers' names," the bartender said, interrupting him. "What's he look like?"

"He's tall, close to fifty, dark hair peppered with gray, and he looks like he'd bite your head off if you tried to buy him a drink.''

"Is he known as the Diamond Gun?"

"I thought you didn't know your customers' names?"

"This one I know," the bartender said. "He's in jail."

"Jail? For what?"

"He killed a man here tonight, shot another, and the sheriff took him to jail."

"Tell me about it."

Clint drank half the beer while listening and, when the man's story was done, said, "Thanks," and headed for the door.

"Ain't you gonna finish your beer?"

The man sitting with his head on the table looked up and said, "I'll finish it."

Clint found the sheriff's office and entered without knocking.

"You the sheriff?" he asked the man seated behind the desk.

"That's right," the man replied, somewhat defiantly. "What do you want?"

Clint stared at the man who, seated, seemed to be smaller than average in size. Diamond surely must have gone with this diminutive lawman willingly.

"You've got a man named Diamond, Ron Diamond?"

"That's right," the lawman said, "the Diamond Gun. What's it to you?"

"We're traveling together."

"So?"

"So why is he in jail?"

"He killed a man."

"And what was that man doing when he killed him?"

"Ain't for me to say," the lawman said. "Your friend

will have to see the judge in the morning.''

"The way I heard the story Diamond fired in self-defense, while facing three men.''

"The way I heard it he already had his gun drawn and fired before the other man, Cleon James, had a chance to draw.''

"Isn't that how he got his reputation?'' Clint asked. "By firing before the other man had a chance to draw?''

"Ain't for me to say.''

"Sheriff—''

"Who are you, anyway?''

"My name's Clint Adams—''

"The Gunsmith?'' the sheriff asked, gaping.

"That's right.''

"And you two are traveling together?''

"That's right.''

"Well,'' the sheriff said, stiffening his jaw, "I don't care who you are or who he is; your friend is gonna have to see the judge.''

"Can I see him now?''

"It's past visiting hours,'' the lawman said.

Clint knew that he could lift the man out of the chair and shake him if he wanted to, but that wasn't going to do any good.

"Sheriff, what have you got against him and me?''

"Don't like gunmen is all.''

"Is that a fact?''

"And I ain't afraid of you,'' the man said belligerently, his voice quavering just a little.

Proving the little man wrong wouldn't accomplish anything. He and Diamond were just going to have to wait until morning to face the judge.

"All right,'' Clint said, "have it your way. What time will you take him to court?''

"Ten o'clock.''

"I'll be here," Clint said, moving toward the door. "Pleasant dreams."

After Clint left the sheriff's office, he walked to the hotel, his mind split between Nancy Sharpe's problem and Ron Diamond's. He hoped that Nancy would understand which was the more important of the two.

The next morning Clint rose with the sun and went looking for the Tyler brothers and, since they were strangers drifting through town, he found them staying in the same hotel he was in.

They were on the same floor, down at the end of the hall. He knocked on their door, and when one of the brothers answered, he pushed the door open violently, throwing the man backward and off balance.

As he stepped into the room, he saw the second brother on the bed, one arm in a sling and reaching awkwardly for his gun, which was hanging on the bedpost, with the other one.

"Don't try it, friend," he said, and the man froze.

"Who the hell are you?" the man on the floor demanded. "What do you want?"

"My name is Clint Adams, boys," Clint said. "Maybe you've heard of me."

The man on the bed said, "Jesus." They had heard of him—which would make his task a lot easier.

At 10:05 all of the principals were present in court and told their stories. Having the most bearing on the case were the remarks made by the Tyler boys, who swore that Diamond had fired in self-defense—which was the exact opposite of what they had told the sheriff the night before. Of course, they had since been visited by the Gunsmith.

●   ●   ●

"I get the feeling," Ron Diamond said, while strapping on his recently returned gunbelt out in front of the courthouse, "that you had something to do with my not being charged."

"I simply visited the Tyler boys and impressed upon them the importance of telling the truth."

"That's what I figured."

At that point the Tyler boys rode past on their horses, heading out of town at full speed.

"And also how important it would be for them to leave town immediately."

The sheriff left the courthouse at that point, gave both Clint and Diamond dirty looks, and then headed for his office, taking quick little steps with his short legs.

"I think it's about time we left this town behind," Diamond said.

"Uh, maybe not," Clint said.

THIRTEEN

The two ranchers whose names Nancy had given Clint were Kyle Webster, of the KW Brand, and William X. Payton, of the WXP Brand. Neither man appeared to be very imaginative, but they were the two wealthiest ranchers in the area.

Clint went to see Kyle Webster.

Ron Diamond went to see William X. Payton, although he said only God knew why.

Clint was not all that impressed with the KW ranch. He'd seen bigger and better, but perhaps this was the best that could be found in these parts.

Not that there was anything wrong with it. The house itself seemed large enough to have four or five rooms, and there was enough stock around to indicate that Mr. Webster's holdings were of a major nature; it was just that the way Nancy had talked about these two big, powerful ranchers, he had expected something more ostentatious.

He pulled Duke to a halt in front of the house and waited while several hands decided who was going to approach him. Finally, a decision was made.

"Can I help you?" a young man asked.

"I'd like to see Mr. Webster."

"He's not here."

"When will he be back?"

"Not for a while," the man replied. "He's off on a buying trip."

"Who's in charge while he's gone?"

The man shrugged and said, "Depends."

"On what?"

"If you're looking for a job, you gotta talk to the foreman, Ike Carter. If it's something else, then I guess you gotta talk to Mrs. Webster."

"I'll talk to Mrs. Webster."

"I'll see if she'll talk to you."

Clint waited astride Duke while the man went into the house, shutting the door behind him. He watched the house and eventually saw a curtain drawn aside and a face appear. It was a woman's face, but beyond that he couldn't tell very much. After another moment, the man reappeared.

"She'll see you. Come this way."

Clint dismounted and dropped Duke's reins to the ground.

"Want somebody to look after him?" the man asked, eyeing Duke hopefully.

"He won't go anywhere."

The man shrugged and led Clint into the house. They entered the house through a large living room, which was well furnished, and he followed the man farther until he came to a closed door.

"Mr. Webster's office," the man said, knocking.

"Come in," a woman's voice called. The man opened the door, entered, and stepped aside to let Clint in.

"That's all, Dave."

"Yes, ma'am."

Dave left, closing the door behind him, and Clint took a moment to study the woman behind the desk.

She was in her mid-forties; her dark hair was streaked with gray and worn shaggy. Her face was handsome and had probably always been so. She looked like what a rancher or businessman's wife should look like—competent.

"What is your name?" she asked.

"Clint Adams."

"You have some business with my husband?"

"Since he's not here, I guess I have some business with you."

"You don't know my husband?"

"No, Mrs. Webster, I've never met your husband. In fact, until yesterday I had never heard of him or of this ranch."

"Why are you here, then?"

"It's about a piece of land that your husband and William Payton are trying to buy."

"Are you here because of that orphanage?" the woman asked.

"Yes, I'm here on behalf of Nancy Sharpe."

"My name is Clint Adams," he repeated.

"And what is your business, Mr. Adams?" she asked, apparently unaware of who he was.

"I'm a gunsmith."

"And how would this business bring you into contact with Nancy Sharpe and her orphanage?"

"Mrs. Webster, none of this is relevant. I stopped a fight involving one of her boys, brought him home, stayed for dinner, and was asked to help."

"And what did she promise you if you helped, huh?" Mrs. Webster asked. She came out from behind the desk and approached him, hands on swaying hips. "I know it couldn't have been money."

"I'm just doing the children a favor, trying to save their home."

"She tried that sad story on my husband, Mr. Adams, and it didn't work. I'm much less susceptible to it."

"That's a shame, Mrs. Webster, because those children

really do need a home more than your husband needs that little plot of land.''

She was about to speak when she stopped as if suddenly struck by something.

"Were you sent here by Payton?" she asked.

"No, ma'am. In fact, a friend of mine is visiting Mr. Payton for the same reason I'm here."

"Which is what, exactly?"

"To try to persuade the two of you that you don't need that land."

"Who are you to say that?"

"Like I told you, Mrs. Webster," Clint said, growing impatient with the woman, "I'm just passing through."

"Well," she said, turning and returning to her desk, "just keep on passing, Mr. Adams. This is none of your concern."

"Do you have any children, Mrs. Webster?"

"No," she said. "Why?"

"I didn't think so."

She frowned, trying to decide if she had been insulted or not, but he didn't give her a chance to reply. "I understand there have been some threats made—"

"Threats?" she asked.

"And some innuendo to Mrs. Sharpe and to the children. You can make as many offers for that land as you please, Mrs. Webster," Clint said, "but threats have no place in business, especially not when they are directed at women and children."

"I'm a woman, Mr. Adams," she said. "Are you threatening me?"

"I'm giving you some damned good advice, ma'am," Clint said, moving for the door. "Do yourself a favor and take it."

•   •   •

Ron Diamond was having no better luck with William X. Payton, a man of some sixty years who, when Diamond was ushered into his office, was sitting in a chair that had wheels.

"I'm sorry I cannot rise to greet you like a man, young fella, but as you can see, that's just not possible."

From that moment on, Diamond felt he was in trouble.

Briefly, Diamond explained that he was there on behalf of the orphanage to try to persuade Payton that he didn't really need that small plot of land.

"Sir, I am not in the habit of discussing my business with strangers, which is precisely what you are. I would like you to leave."

"Look—" Diamond began to say and then he stopped short. He'd been about to say Old Man. But just how much older than he was the rancher?

"Look, Mr. Payton," Diamond said, "I respect your right to try to make a purchase, but do not do it by threatening a woman and some children."

"I don't know what you're talking about," Payton said. "If I were not stuck in this chair, I would get up and throw you out myself."

"I'm going, Mr. Payton," Diamond said, "but remember what I said. Harassing women and children is the work of a coward."

"You have the nerve to speak to me of cowardice?" the man in the chair demanded, his face turning very red. "It is an act of courage simply to go on living each day in this blasted chair! Don't talk to me about cowardice. Get out. Get out, damn you!"

For a moment Diamond thought that Payton would rise from the chair, but he backed out of the room before the man had a heart attack.

● ● ●

"The old man is just too bitter to care," Diamond told Clint.

"And the woman is out to prove something," Clint said. "I wonder if I might not have made better headway with her husband."

They were in the Half Dollar Saloon, and each had relayed his experience to the other.

"What more can we do, Clint?" Diamond asked.

"I don't know," Clint said, "but there must be something."

"Look," Diamond said, "I went along with this because you got me out of some trouble, but I don't have the time to waste here, Clint."

"I know," Clint said. "I'll go out and talk to Nancy and meet you back here."

"Maybe I ought to come with you," Diamond offered.

"Don't you think I can handle a woman?"

"Handle, yes," Diamond said, "but say no to?"

Clint decided not to mention Belinda and simply rose and left the saloon.

Mrs. Lucy Webster looked down at Ike Carter and then brushed her full, naked breasts against his face. The foreman's tongue flicked out to pass over her nipples, causing her to shiver, and then he bit one and she laughed happily.

"What did that fella want, Lucille?" Ike Carter asked.

Seated astride the foreman and with his stiffened cock pinned beneath her, she asked, "Are you jealous?"

"He was in with you for a long time."

"Darling," she said, rubbing her hands over his hairy chest. Her husband, Kyle, was in his fifties and was so flabby he appeared to have breasts. Ike Carter, on the other hand, was thirty-three and hard as a rock and was very eager to please his employer's wife.

"He came to argue for that woman at the orphanage."

"She's hired herself a gunman?" he asked in surprise.

"What do you mean a gunman?"

"Dave told me he thought he recognized the fella. What was his name?"

She thought a moment and then said, "Adams, Clint Adams."

"Jesus, Lucille," Carter said, "do you know who that is?"

"No, who?"

"That is the Gunsmith."

"The Gunsmith," she repeated. She hadn't recognized the name Adams, but she knew this name—and he'd had the nerve to say he was a gunsmith.

"We may have to escalate our plan to get that piece of land, darling," she said.

"Whatever you say, Lucille."

"You're not afraid of the Gunsmith?" she asked, rubbing herself up and down the length of his shaft.

"I'd do anything for you, baby."

"Mmmm, anything?" she asked.

"You know it," he said. He slid his hands beneath her to cup her wide buttocks, lifted her, and then eased her down on his shaft. She was so slick that he slid in easily.

Ike Carter felt that by fucking Lucille and keeping her happy he was assuring himself of a piece of the action somewhere down the road. Even though she was a little over the hill, the fact that she was so energetic in bed and liked sex so much—and didn't get any from her husband—made this task that much easier to take.

"Mr. Payton?"

Payton looked up from his desk and saw his foreman's head peering at him from behind the door.

"Yes, what is it, Casey?"

"Just something I thought you should know, sir."

"All right, come in."

"Yes, sir."

Casey Freeman approached the desk cautiously. A tall, raw-boned man in his forties, Freeman virtually ran the ranch for Payton, who had not been able to walk since falling off a horse six years earlier—a horse he never should have been on.

"Well, what is it?"

"The man who was here earlier, sir."

"What about him?"

"Did he give you his name?"

"I didn't give him a chance to," Payton said. "I don't discuss my business with strangers, Casey. You know that."

"Yes, sir, I surely do—but it occurs to me that you should know who that man is."

"What are you talking about?"

"I recognized him, Mr. Payton. I saw him ten years ago and, even though he's changed some and is supposed to be dead, I knew him when I saw him."

"What are you going on about?" Payton asked, annoyed. "Spit it out!"

"His name's Ron Diamond, Mr. Payton. People call him the Diamond Gun."

"A gunman?" Payton asked in disbelief.

"Yes, sir."

"That orphanage woman has hired herself a gunman? We'll have to do something about that, Casey."

"I guess—"

"I know you're sweet on that woman, Casey, but business is business."

"I know that, sir. I always put the welfare of the ranch ahead of my personal life."

"And I appreciate it, Casey. I really do."

"Thank you, sir."

"Now, if she's bringing in a gunman, then we've got him to worry about as well as Webster. We're going to have to move up our timetable, Casey. I want that land!"

The old man slammed his fist down on the desk and Casey said, "I know you do, sir."

Casey Freeman, on the other hand, wanted Nancy Sharpe and the only way he knew of getting her was to take the orphanage away from her so she'd have to come to him to be taken care of. She was too independent now, but without that orphanage . . .

"And we'll get it, sir. Count on it."

FOURTEEN

As Clint rode out to the orphanage, Diamond went to the general store to stock up on supplies that he and Clint would need when they left town.

Upon entering the store, Diamond saw a lovely girl of about eighteen making a purchase, and with her were three small children, a boy and two girls. One of the girls had dark pigtails and dark skin and reminded him very much of Delores.

He found it difficult to keep his eyes off the little girl and was only vaguely aware when two men entered the store.

"I'll be with you as soon as I help the young lady," the storekeeper said to Diamond.

"No rush."

He was in the back of the store examining some merchandise when the other two men stepped forward and pushed aside the young girl. One of the men shoved past the children and sent the little dark-haired girl sprawling to the floor.

"The Payton ranch gives you most of your business, Elijah," one man said, "so you better take care of us first."

Diamond rushed to the fallen little girl and picked her up off the floor. She smiled at him and reminded him even more of his dead wife.

The young woman came to his side and said, "Thank you," taking the little girl from him.

"Stay here," he told her as the other two children rushed to her side.

"Well, come on, Elijah," one of the men said.

"You men need to learn some manners."

The two men turned from the counter and looked at Diamond, obviously unimpressed by what they saw. They were both in their twenties, both over six feet, and both full of themselves.

"You talking to us, friend?"

"You should know better than to push children around, fellas."

"Anybody who gets in the way gets pushed, friend," one man said. "You're getting pretty close to that right now."

"If you want to push me, friend, you'd better get some help," Diamond said. "It's going to take more than two of you."

The spokesman looked over at his friend, who was grinning.

"What do you think, Wade? Are we gonna need more help?"

"I don't think so."

The two men began to step forward. "Not that way, son," Diamond said. "I'm not about to try to trade fists with two young bucks."

"You mean you want to shoot it out over some orphaned kids?"

"That's up to you fellas, isn't it? Either go for your guns or walk out."

Now the two men did not seem so sure of themselves, and their resolve was visibly faltering.

"Look, friend—"

"You," Diamond said, pointing to the man who had knocked the little girl down and who had not yet spoken. "Even if you walk out of here, be watching for me."

"What did I do?"

"You like to knock down little girls."

"Look, mister—"

"No more talk."

The two men looked into the eyes of the older man and both shivered.

"Let's go, Wade," the spokesman said, and both of them moved toward the door, slowly at first and then faster until they were out.

Diamond looked at the storekeeper and said, "You'd better finish waiting on these kids."

"I'm not a kid," the young woman said, stepping forward.

Diamond looked at her and saw a beautiful, sensuous young woman who, to him, was still a child, no matter how grown up she looked or thought she was.

"Excuse me," he said. "Take care of the young lady, please," he said to the storekeeper.

"With pleasure," the man said.

Diamond crouched down so he could talk to the dark-haired little girl.

"What's your name, honey?"

"Lisa. What's yours?"

"Ron."

"This is Mary and Kevin," she said, introducing the two other children.

"Hello," Diamond said to them, but his attention was on the little girl. He couldn't help thinking that if Delores had lived and had a baby girl, she would have looked like this little girl.

"Thank you for your help, Ron," she said to him.

"You're welcome, honey. Did you get hurt when you fell?"

"No, I'm all right."

"Well, when you've got everything you came for, Lisa, I'll take you and your friends back to the orphanage."

"They're not my friends," she said.

"They're not?"

"They're my family," Lisa said. "Mrs. Sharpe says we're all family until somebody adopts us. Do you think she meant that after we're adopted we're not family anymore?"

"I think you'll always be family to each other, Lisa."

"I hope so," Lisa said. "I like having so many brothers and sisters . . . but I would like to have a mother and father."

"I'm sure you would."

"Do you have any children?"

"No, honey, I don't."

"Maybe you should come out to the orphanage, Ron," Lisa said, "and you might like one of us."

"Maybe I should, Lisa," Diamond said. "Maybe I should."

FIFTEEN

Clint had ridden out toward the Duneden Orphanage, and just out of town he had passed Belinda and three children taking a buckboard into town. Belinda had sent a dazzling smile his way, and the memory of her naked sent a tightening sensation into his groin and caused him to be even more impressed with his own willpower.

When he reached the orphanage, he left Duke out front, mounted the porch, and knocked. The door was answered by a small boy and Clint told him that he'd like to see Mrs. Sharpe.

"She's in the kitchen," the towheaded lad said. "I'll get her."

"Thank you."

The boy ran off, and after a few moments, Nancy Sharpe appeared at the door, drying her hands on an apron she wore around her waist.

"Hi, Clint."

"Hello, Nancy. Let's talk."

"Of course."

She removed the apron, tossed it aside, and then came out to the porch, closing the door behind her.

"Did you talk to them?" she asked eagerly. "Mr. Webster and Mr. Payton?"

"Mr. Webster is away on a buying trip, Nancy," Clint said. "I talked to Mrs. Webster."

"That bitch!" Nancy said with vehemence so sudden it surprised Clint. "We don't like each other, Clint, and I think perhaps she's the one behind Webster's desire for this land."

"And Payton?"

"He's a bitter old man who needs little excuse to cause others trouble. When he heard that Webster wanted the land, he decided he wanted it as well. Did you see him?"

"My friend did and he agrees with you, Nancy. Payton's a bitter old man."

"Then you couldn't talk either one out of it?" she asked. "That's all it would take, you know. If Webster would decide he didn't want the land, Payton wouldn't want it."

"According to what you say, that would mean convincing Mrs. Webster to dislike you less."

"Not much chance of that," Nancy said, folding her arms across her breasts.

"You didn't tell me there was something personal in this, Nancy."

"There isn't on my part—or there wasn't. I don't know. We saw each other on the street one day, and she seemed to take an instant dislike to me."

"Maybe you took the attention away from her. She can't stand to have a young, more beautiful woman in town, especially when her own looks are fading."

"Do you think that's it?"

"I've seen her and I've seen you, Nancy," Clint said, "and it's no competition."

She grinned slightly and said, "Thank you."

"Obviously, you're not that kind of woman."

"What do you mean?"

"If you couldn't stand the competition, you wouldn't keep Belinda around."

"Belinda," Nancy said, shaking her head. "She's a child."

"Not such a child," Clint said, and when Nancy looked at him sharply, he changed the subject.

"Nancy, I don't know what else I can do. My friend and I can't—"

He was interrupted by the sound of an approaching buckboard. They spotted Belinda and the children coming toward the house, and Clint was surprised to find that they were being accompanied by Ron Diamond.

"Who is that?" Nancy asked.

"That's my friend, Ron Diamond."

When they reached the house, Diamond dismounted and helped Belinda and the children down. Clint noticed the dark-haired little girl and noticed how Diamond held her a little longer than the others. As she mounted the porch and walked past him to Nancy, he was shocked at her resemblance to Delores Rondo.

"Ron helped us in town, Nancy. He made some men leave us alone."

"Belinda?" Nancy said.

"I'll tell you about it, Nancy," Belinda said with a glance at Clint.

"Clint, why don't you give me a hand unloading this wagon?" Diamond called out.

"Excuse me," Clint said to Nancy.

When he reached the buckboard, he saw that there weren't really enough supplies to require two men to unload, so Diamond had something else on his mind. Nancy ushered Belinda and the children into the house, leaving the door open for Clint and Diamond to follow.

"What's on your mind, Ron?" Clint asked as they approached the door.

"Did you tell Mrs. Sharpe that we were leaving?"

"Not yet. I was about to when you arrived."

"Good," Diamond said. He stopped on the porch and

said, "I think we should stay and help these children, Clint. We can't leave them to face this trouble alone."

"This is a change of heart, Ron."

"I've just done some thinking, that's all."

"What about your . . . business?"

"Maybe this won't take long."

Clint decided he knew what had changed Diamond's mind and decided not to pursue it.

"All right, Ron," he said. "We'll stay and help them."

"And after, we'll take up the hunt again," Diamond said.

"If that's what you want, Ron," Clint said, but as Diamond entered the house ahead of him, he wondered if it was indeed what Diamond would want later.

Clint and Diamond stayed for lunch, and Diamond sat next to Lisa at the table. Even over the course of that short meal, Clint could see a bond forming between the two of them—or at least for Diamond.

On the other hand, Belinda sat next to Clint, across from Nancy, and Clint couldn't tell if Nancy knew what was going on. Belinda's hand was on his knee and then his thigh, and rather than start a ruckus at the table, he would save some choice words for the young lady later.

After lunch, the children all helped to clear the table, and Nancy invited Clint and Diamond to wait for her in the sitting room.

"There's some brandy there."

They went to the sitting room and Clint poured two glasses of brandy. As he handed one to Diamond, the man looked at him and nodded. "You know, don't you?" Diamond asked.

"She does bear a striking resemblance to Delores, Ron."

"And to the child we would have had."

"I'm sorry . . ."

"Don't be sorry, Clint. Just see if you can keep me from making a fool out of myself." Diamond got a faraway look in his eyes and said, "I don't mind staying here to help them, but after that, keep me from making a fool out of myself."

Clint wasn't sure what Diamond meant, but at that point Nancy came into the room. Clint poured her a brandy and handed it to her.

"I suppose you gentlemen will be leaving Duneden now," she said, sitting down.

"No, Nancy," Clint said, "we've talked it over and have decided to stay and help. We won't leave until this problem of yours is all cleared up."

She smiled at both of them and said, "I'm glad, Clint. Thank you. Thank both of you."

"Thanks can come later," Clint said. "Right now, we'd better decide what our next move is."

SIXTEEN

Their first move was to move into the orphanage. They returned to town, checked out of the hotel, and returned with all of their belongings.

After dinner they were shown to their rooms. The building had two floors, and there were empty rooms on each. They were given their choice. Clint felt they should stay on different floors in order to cover the entire building. Diamond agreed.

Clint took an upstairs room and Diamond a downstairs one. The choice was arbitrarily made, and the coincidences involved would come to light on that first night.

The first coincidence was that Lisa had a room on the first floor, one door away from Diamond's. It served to illustrate further that fate might be bringing the two of them together.

The second coincidence became apparent to Clint during the night.

When the door to his room opened, he had his gun hanging on his bedpost, but he instinctively knew that he wouldn't be needing it.

"Clint."

The voice was low, young, and unmistakably female.

"Clint."

She came closer to the bed, and then she knelt on it. He

could smell her, then; she had a young, clean, fresh smell that he reacted to.

It was Belinda. She pulled his covers back and he turned over to face her, to stop her.

"Belinda, don't—"

She slid off the bed, stepped back, and dropped her nightgown to the floor. By the moonlight coming through the window, he could see her breasts, her belly button, the triangle of light hair between her legs. Mingled with her fresh, clean smell was the scent of her readiness, which he especially reacted to.

"Clint—" she said, putting her knee on the bed again.

"Belinda, this isn't right—"

"Shhh," she said, putting her finger against his lips, "Nancy's room is on this floor. You don't want to wake her, do you?"

"Is that your game?"

"I don't think of it as a game," she said, sliding underneath his covers. He felt her body against his and all thoughts of resistance faded. Her breasts were small but firm, and her nipples pressed against him through his longjohns. Her hands quickly undid his underwear and delved inside, finding him hard and ready.

"Oh, yes . . ." she whispered, and with his help she divested him of his underclothing, stripping him naked.

Her lips started at his chest and worked down over his belly until they closed over him, taking him inside her mouth. His hands cupped her head as she suckled him, and he wondered where this young woman had learned to do so well what she was doing.

Later, she climbed atop him, steadied him with her hand, and impaled herself on him. She rode him wildly, and all the while, they both fought to keep silent, lest they wake up Nancy or any of the others in the house.

Afterward, she lay in the crook of his arm. "Before morning I'll have to go back to my own room," she said, "but I can come to you every night."

"No."

"No?" she said, her hand moving to grasp his semierect penis. "You don't want me?"

"You know that's not it."

"You want Nancy?"

"That's not it either, damn it."

"She wants you. Did you know that?"

"Belinda, you're very young—"

"Not so young," she said, squeezing him.

"We'll have to talk about this."

"Sure, tonight."

"No, in the open somewhere."

"Coward," she said, swinging her legs to the floor and standing up. He watched—he couldn't help himself—as she slipped into her nightgown again.

"We'll talk, Clint," she said and sneaked from his room back to hers.

Clint wondered if he'd gotten himself into more than he could handle.

Old Man Payton had sent for his foreman, Casey Freeman, who was now standing in front of his desk.

"I want you to go to town, Casey, and send this telegram," the old man said, handing him a piece of paper with some of Payton's writing on it. Freeman, practiced at reading the man's handwriting, was able to decipher it and looked doubtfully at his employer.

"Do you think this is wise, Mr. Payton?"

"What's unwise about it?" Payton retorted. "That woman has hired herself a gunman; I got the right to hire one myself."

"But, sir, even though Ron Diamond has been out of circulation for a while, do you think that this man could handle him?"

"That man," Payton said, nodding his head at the piece of paper Freeman held in his hand, "is twenty years younger than this Diamond and is said to be lightning-quick with a gun."

"But sir, he doesn't have the reputation that Ron Diamond has—"

"Precisely why I'm sending for him," Payton said, interrupting his foreman. "He's a Wyoming product, so he's nearby, and he'll be hungry to make a reputation for himself. When he learns that the Diamond Gun is here in Duneden, he'll come running."

"I don't doubt that."

"Then send that telegram and stop dawdling, Casey. I'm just protecting my interest. What do you think Webster's gonna do when he hears there's a gunman involved? Sit on his hands?"

Payton thought again and then said, "Well, he might, but that devil he's married to won't. Damn, if she don't light a fire under that man every once in a while."

The old man got a wistful look in his eyes and said, "She'd light a fire under me, too, if it wasn't for this damned chair. Is she still messing with that foreman of hers?"

"I don't know, sir."

The old man got a faraway look in his eyes and said, "I love a woman with a wide bottom, boy."

"Yes, sir," Freeman said. "I'll send the telegram first thing in the morning."

"That's what I told you to do, ain't it?"

"Yes, sir."

"Then get to it!"

As Freeman left the old man was grinning and muttering, "I do like a woman with a wide bottom, yes sir!"

At that precise moment, Lucille Webster was putting her wide bottom to good use, riding Ike Carter for all she was worth. Holding the generous cheeks of her ass in his big hands, Carter thought that he had never met a woman who liked being on top so damn much.

Her body shook with orgasm and he watched as the cords in her neck stood out. He was always amazed at how she never made a sound when she came. He wasn't that quiet, and as he climaxed, a great groan escaped from him and he came like a waterfall.

"Ike?" she asked moments later.

"Yep?"

"Do you think I should send for someone?"

"You mean I ain't enough for you anymore, baby?" he asked, pinching her plump thigh.

"You're plenty enough man for me, Ike," she said, rubbing her hand over his hairy chest, "but I'm talking about someone to handle Clint Adams."

"You mean a hired gun?"

"Do you know anybody?"

Carter thought a moment and then said, "I might know someone, yeah, but I don't know as this is such a good idea, Lucille."

"I've got to protect myself, Ike, and I've got to protect Kyle's interests while he's away. If he doesn't trust me, he won't go away so much on these buying trips of his, and you and I won't be able to be together as much."

Ike Carter knew just the answer she wanted, and he gave it to her.

"Well, by all means, sweetie, I'll send for someone first

thing in the morning. After all, we've got to make sure that old Kyle goes right on trusting you, don't we?''

He rolled on top of her then, and as she grabbed for him with both hands he hoped she'd at least let him be on top this time.

SEVENTEEN

The next morning it was Casey Freeman who got to the telegraph office first and sent his telegram. As he left, he was observed by Ike Carter who went inside, sent his telegram off, and then paid the clerk fifty cents to let him see Freeman's. Once he learned that Payton was also sending for a gun, he rushed back to the ranch to tell Lucille. Not only was that woman fine in bed, she also had a good head on her shoulders and generally came up with the right ideas.

It seemed that she had done it again this time because she surely was going to need someone for protection.

Casey Freeman, while leaving the telegraph office, saw Ike Carter out of the corner of an eye, but did not let on that he had. After Carter had rushed out of the office, Freeman went back in and paid the clerk fifty cents for a look at Carter's telegram.

Armed with the knowledge that Lucille Webster was sending for a gunman, he headed back to the Payton ranch as fast as his horse could carry him with that information, feeling that the old man was now justified in sending for help.

When Clint woke the sheets of his bed still held the fragrance of Belinda and of their lovemaking, and he hastily made the bed himself, lest Nancy come in to do it for him and notice the odors.

In the kitchen he found the brood assembled for breakfast, with Diamond sitting next to little Lisa. There were two other chairs available, one next to Belinda and the other next to the boy, Todd. Clint chose to sit next to the boy—to Todd's delight and Belinda's well-disguised disappointment.

"Well, did you gentlemen sleep well last night?" Nancy asked.

"Just fine, ma'am," Diamond answered.

She looked at Clint and he wondered if he didn't look a little guilty.

"I slept all right, thanks."

"I slept marvelously," Belinda spoke up.

Nancy looked at her and said, "Really?"

"Oh, I can't think when I've had a better night, Nancy," Belinda said with a quick glance at Clint.

"Well, what would you attribute that to, Belinda?" Nancy asked.

"Oh, maybe it's because we had these two gentlemen in the house, Nancy, and I felt so safe."

Again she cast a glance Clint's way, one he was sure everyone at the table must have noticed.

"Well, I must admit," Nancy said, "I did feel a bit safer myself for your presence, Clint . . . and Ron."

"Glad to oblige, ma'am," Diamond said.

Although Clint felt sure that Nancy must have sensed something between him and Belinda, he noticed that most of Nancy's attention seemed to be on Ron Diamond and Lisa. He was prepared, then, for her questions afterward while the others were cleaning up.

"Clint, about your friend . . . I'm concerned about the amount of attention he's giving Lisa."

"There's nothing sinister in it, Nancy," Clint assured her.

"Well, I didn't think so," she protested, although he was

sure the thought must have entered her mind. Lisa was such a pretty little girl.

"Delores, Ron's wife, was killed a short time ago. She was a lovely woman with dark hair, dark eyes, and dark skin."

"Oh."

"And she was carrying their child."

"Oh!"

"If she had lived and had a baby girl, I think the baby would have looked much like Lisa."

"Oh, I see," Nancy said. "I feel so foolish. Thank you, Clint, for telling me that."

"Just don't let Ron know I told you, Nancy."

"No, of course I won't."

"Good."

"Uh, may I say something else?"

"Of course."

"I've noticed that Belinda is giving you quite a lot of attention."

"Uh—"

"I believe she has a crush on you."

"Really?"

"Yes. She's a young woman now, Clint, so I would appreciate it if you would handle her delicately. Try not to bruise her ego."

"Well, I'll sure try, Nancy. I wouldn't want to hurt her in any way."

"I knew I could count on you," she said, putting a hand on his arm.

He looked down at her hand and said, "And what about you?"

"I beg your pardon?"

"Do you have a crush on anyone?"

"Oh," she said, taking her hand away. "Do you mean do I have a man friend?"

"I suppose that's what I mean."

"Well, at the moment no . . . although there is a man who has shown some interest in me."

"Really?"

"His name is Casey Freeman; he's the foreman at Mr. Payton's ranch."

"I see. And how do you feel about him?"

"I'm afraid I can't reciprocate, especially since it is his employer who is trying to force us off this land, and his coworkers who are being ugly about it."

"Well, maybe this gives us a place to start."

"What do you mean?"

"Maybe I should have a talk with Casey Freeman. If he feels so strongly about you, maybe he can help persuade Mr. Payton that he doesn't need this little piece of land."

"I don't know, Clint," Nancy said, looking dubious. "Casey is quite loyal to Mr. Payton."

"Well, we'll find out what's stronger," Clint said, his tone teasing, "his loyalty or his lust."

"Lust!" Nancy said, coloring slightly. "I'd hardly call it that!"

Clint gave her a very deliberate look and said, "Well, I would!"

Lisa had been able to persuade Ron Diamond to help clear the table and do the dishes. Clint was waiting for him in the sitting room when he came out.

"I thought I asked you to keep me from making a fool out of myself," Diamond said.

"Doing a few dishes won't hurt you," Clint said. "Listen, I'm going out to the Payton ranch."

"What for?"

Clint told Diamond what Nancy had told him about the Payton foreman.

"Can't say that I blame the man," Diamond said. "She's a fine woman."

"Yes, she is."

"So's that young one, what's her name?"

"Belinda."

"Yes. Seems to me you've got your hands full, friend."

"What are you talking about?"

"Both of those gals seem to have their minds set on you, and they're both sure enough to keep you busy."

"Belinda is a child," Clint said, feeling foolish as he said it. She'd proved to him just last night that she wasn't such a child.

"Not such a child," Diamond said. "I'll saddle up and come with you."

"I don't think you should."

"Why not?"

"Payton knows you."

"So does his foreman," Diamond added. "He is the one who took me in to see the old man."

"All the more reason you should stay behind. If they see me riding up with you, they'll get close-mouthed right off. I want to see if I can find out just how much store this Freeman fella sets by Nancy. Maybe we can use it."

"What am I supposed to do in the meantime?"

"Stay around here," Clint suggested. "Do more house-work. Hey, bake a cake, why don't you?"

Diamond frowned and said, "Thanks."

After Clint had left, Lisa and Belinda came into the sitting room looking for Diamond.

"There you are," Lisa said, running to him and grabbing his hand. As soon as she touched him, he was lost.

"Hi, sweetheart, I was just saying good-bye to Clint."

"Is he going away?"

"For a little while, but he'll be back."

"Are you staying?"

"Sure I am."

"Oh, good!" she said. She released his hand only long enough to clap hers together and then reclaimed it.

"Ron, can I ask you something?" Belinda said.

"Sure, Belinda."

"Have you known Clint long?"

"On and off for some time. Why? Are you setting your sights on him?"

"I might be."

"I wouldn't advise that."

"Why?"

"Well, for one thing he's a lot older than you."

"That's not a good reason," she said and then added, "Why, how old is he?"

"Well, he's not that far from my age."

"Oh, he couldn't be that old!"

"Thanks a lot."

She touched his arm, laughing, and said, "That's not what I meant."

"Sure it is, but that's all right. Were you two looking for me?"

"Yes."

"Why?"

"Lisa wants you to help us."

"Do what?"

"Bake a cake."

"It'll be fun!" Lisa said.

Diamond pasted a smile on his face and said, "I'm sure it will, honey."

EIGHTEEN

Clint rode out to the Payton ranch, wondering if the appearance of a stranger for a second day in a row would be unusual. He hadn't quite decided how he would go into this, whether he would pretend he was looking for a job or simply be straightforward with the foreman, Casey Freeman.

He did not ride right up to the house—wanting to avoid a meeting with Payton himself—but rather rode to the corral where a trio of cowhands stood, discussing whatever it is cowhands discuss early in the morning.

"Morning."

They all looked up and, while two of them simply nodded, the third inclined his head and said, "Good morning. Can I help you?"

"You can if you're Casey Freeman."

"I am."

"Can we talk in private?"

Freeman turned to the other men and told them to get on about their work. As they walked away, the foreman—as tall as Clint, but almost ten years younger—walked up to Duke and examined him.

"You wouldn't be wanting to part with this horse, would you?"

"Not a chance."

"I'll offer you a good price."

"I didn't come here to try to sell my horse."

"That's what I was afraid of."

Clint found the man studying him strangely and decided to dismount and talk with him on even ground.

"What was it you wanted to talk about?"

"Nancy Sharpe."

Freeman frowned and asked, "What's your interest in Nancy Sharpe."

"I'm trying to help her with a problem she seems to have."

"What kind of problem, mister? How well do you know Miss Nancy?"

"Not very well, I admit, but she did ask me to help out, and I'm just trying to oblige."

"Why would she ask you?"

"Guess I just happened to be available."

"And what would this problem be exactly."

"Seems there are two big ranchers in the area trying to force her to sell the land her orphanage is sitting on. It seems they're using questionable means."

"What's that got to do with me?"

"Well, I heard you set some store by Nancy," Clint said, watching the man's face. A muscle started to jump along the man's right jawline. "I figured maybe I could get you to help her."

"She send you here?"

"No, but she knew I was coming. She warned me I was wasting my time, that you were too loyal to your employer."

"Miss Nancy knows me pretty well, then."

"Maybe I was mistaken about the way you felt about her."

"You weren't mistaken, but one's got nothing to do with the other."

"You mean, you'd stand by and watch her being stampeded off her land?"

The muscles in Freeman's shoulders tensed and he said, "Mister, I don't see as I have to be discussing this with you. You never even introduced yourself."

"I'm sorry about that," Clint said. "My name's Clint Adams."

As tense as the foreman was, he got a whole lot more so when he heard the name.

"The Gunsmith?"

"I've been called that."

"What's Nancy trying to do, start a war?"

"What do you mean?"

"First, she hires the Diamond Gun and now the Gunsmith? Seems she's asking for trouble."

"First of all, the way I heard it, the trouble was started by your boss and by Kyle Webster. Second of all, Ron Diamond and I have not hired out to anyone. We're trying to help out here as a favor. We don't want to see those children without a home."

"Paid or not, if you two hang around, there's gonna be big trouble."

"Why?"

"You got reps."

"Reputations can be deceiving, Mr. Freeman," Clint said. He turned, mounted Duke, and looked down at the foreman. "Look at you. You had a rep as a man who cared for a lady, and you're not going to lift a hand to help her."

"I can't."

"Can't and won't are real close, friend," Clint said. "You'd better decide which word you really want to use."

With that Clint wheeled Duke around, then stopped, and turned in his saddle.

"If you want to talk to me, I'll be staying out at the orphanage."

"And Diamond?"

"He's there, too."

"With Nancy?"

"It's her orphanage," Clint said and, turning his back, rode away wondering if he'd managed to accomplish anything positive or done more damage than good.

When Clint reached the point where he was an equal distance from town and from the orphanage, an idea occurred to him. He changed his direction and headed for Duneden. If the town had a telegraph office, he wanted to visit it. Perhaps, with the help of a dollar or two, he could find out if any telegrams had been sent the day before or even that same morning.

Maybe he'd find out something that would help.

Or hurt.

NINETEEN

When Clint returned to the orphanage, he found Ron Diamond in the kitchen wearing an apron and sporting a spot of batter on the tip of his nose.

"Sorry to intrude," he said.

Diamond turned to face Clint and looked at him gratefully. "Need me for something?" he asked hopefully.

"I guess it can wait."

"That's all right," Diamond said, hastily undoing the apron.

"Ron—" Lisa said plaintively.

"I'm sorry, honey," Diamond said, handing a smiling Belinda the apron, "but Clint needs me."

"Will you bring him back?" Lisa asked Clint.

"Just as soon as I can, Lisa."

Diamond took hold of Clint's arm and hustled him out of the kitchen.

"You came back just in time."

"You've got batter on your nose."

Diamond hastily wiped his nose with the back of his hand and said, "What did you find out?"

"From the foreman at the Payton spread, not much. He's

sweet on Nancy, though, so I might have succeeded in firing him up for a different reason.''

"You did find out something, though?"

"Yes."

"What?"

"Both Payton and Mrs. Webster have sent for help, Ron," Clint said. He took two sheets of paper from his pocket and handed them to Diamond.

"What are these?"

"Two telegrams, each sent by a ranch foreman. Cost me a dollar a piece."

"I'll give you half."

"No argument."

Diamond read both telegrams and then handed them back to Clint. "Do you know either one of these fellas?" Ron asked.

"No, not personally or by reputation. From what I could gather from the telegraph operator, one of them is a local product. He doesn't know the other one."

"Maybe we should send some telegrams of our own?" Diamond suggested.

"I already have," Clint said and then went on to explain about his friend Rick Hartman, a saloon owner in Labyrinth, Texas, who had more contacts in the west—and the east— than any man Clint knew.

"If anybody can identify these two fellas for us, Rick can."

"Good," Diamond said, "at least then we'll know what we're up against."

"I guess you can go back to the kitchen now," Clint said, but the remark seemed to go over Diamond's head. Judging from the faraway look in the man's eyes, Clint felt that he was thinking about his dead wife and unborn child.

"Lisa's waiting."

Diamond's eyes focused on Clint's face and he said, "Thanks for the warning."

"Where are you going?"

Almost out the door already, Diamond called back, "To exercise my horse."

Suddenly realizing that in Diamond's absence he might be pressed into kitchen service, Clint called out, "I'll come along with you."

The direction of their ride took them toward town, and they decided to check the telegraph office to see if a reply had come in from Rick Hartman.

"If he had the information at his fingertips," Clint reasoned, "he might have answered already."

And indeed he had.

They retired to the saloon, took two beers to a corner table, and contemplated Hartman's reply.

"The local boy is named Ted Willis," Clint said, reading from the telegram. "He's got a small reputation in Wyoming, and he's looking to expand it."

"Is he any good?"

"According to Rick he's never really been tested," Clint said. "Of course, that doesn't mean that he's not any good."

"And the other one?"

"Rick's heard of him," Clint said. "Taylor Hendry. Here's a surprise. He's an Englishman. He came to this country as a teenager, apparently to escape being hanged in his native England."

"For what?"

"Killing a man in a fight over a woman."

"With a gun?"

Clint nodded.

"With a gun."

"How does your friend Hartman manage to have all of this information?"

"Sometimes I wonder about that myself," Clint said, "but it usually manages to come in handy, so I've never questioned him. I guess he wasn't always a saloon owner."

"I've been out of circulation, Clint, but how come you've never heard of this Hendry?"

"According to Rick, he's only twenty-four," Clint explained, "and he's spent most of his time in this country in the east. He's only come out west recently."

"So what we've got are two hungry wolf cubs looking to make a name for themselves."

"Against two shaggy old wolves like us," Clint added. "I'd guess that young Willis would get here first since he's local."

"And from the address on the telegram to Hendry, he shouldn't be more than a day behind. That means we could take them one at a time."

"Yes," Clint said, "we could."

"It would be the smart thing to do," Diamond said. "There's no telling how good they are."

"You're right," Clint said. "It would be the smart thing to do."

They sipped their beer in silence for a while and then Diamond said, "If we were smart, we wouldn't be in this situation, would we?"

"No, we certainly wouldn't."

Diamond sighed and said, "I guess we're stuck here for a few more days, until those two young bucks get here."

"Who knows?" Clint said. "Since one works for Payton and the other for Webster, they might end up going up against each other and saving us the trouble of dealing with them."

"Sure," Diamond said. "Who knows?"

That would have been the easy way, though, and both men knew that their feet had never—or hardly ever—managed to find the easy path.

TWENTY

Two days went by with Diamond trying to avoid the kitchen—though not trying to avoid Lisa—and Clint trying to avoid Belinda. He had even gone so far as to lock his door at night. The first night he'd heard her at the door. She had tried the knob and then knocked softly, not wanting to wake the rest of the house. Eventually, she had gone away and all the next day had fixed him with hurt looks and glances. The next night she did not try his door.

"What did you say to Belinda?" Nancy asked him on the second night.

"What do you mean?"

It was after dinner, which had become virtually the only time during the day that they spent alone. The others were clearing the table and doing dishes, and Diamond had taken to disappearing after dinner, either to avoid kitchen duty or to be alone with his thoughts.

"She seems hurt or disappointed with you."

"Nancy, I'm not trying to hurt her, but she is very young—"

"I understand," Nancy said, "but she does have a terrible crush on you, Clint."

"Nancy, at her age I think it could be called more than just a crush."

"Really?" she asked, and he caught her looking at him speculatively. Was she beginning to wonder if there wasn't something going on between them? There wasn't, really, except for that one night, and Clint still felt very guilty about that. He hoped that the guilt didn't show too much. There was another kind of guilt involved, though. He felt guilty because he had found himself disappointed that Belinda had not approached his door that second night. Would he have opened it if she had? That was something he hoped he'd never find out.

"I'm going to find Ron, Nancy," he said at that point. "I'll see you later."

On the first day after Clint had heard from Rick, Ted Willis arrived in town. He was dressed in regular trail clothes, and his gun was a well-used .45 that he'd inherited from his father, who had never known how to use it properly. He had given it to a fourteen-year-old Ted Willis, and the youngster had practiced with it day and night. When he had enough money, he planned to buy himself a brand-new weapon.

A tall, gangly youngster with the look of a farm boy, he was riding an old mare who looked as if she'd be more at home pulling a plow, and when he had enough money, he planned on buying himself a new horse.

Barely twenty, Willis had an exaggerated opinion of his own prowess with a gun. He knew how good he was, but nobody else did. This was going to be his chance to prove it to everyone.

Willis arrived in response to Ike Carter's telegram, and would be working for Lucy Webster.

On the next day, Taylor Hendry arrived. He was well dressed in expensive, dark clothing. He wore a black hat and black gloves.

Hendry was a tall, well-formed man with big shoulders and graceful hands. He rode a small, glossy black colt that responded to the slightest pressure of his hands or knees. The liveryman, upon accepting the job of caring for the horse, felt that it was the finest horse he'd ever had the pleasure of caring for—except for that big black gelding belonging to Clint Adams, which was no longer in his care. This one seemed almost like a miniature version of that one, and he felt honored to have had the opportunity to care for two such animals in the same week.

Hendry was responding to Casey Freeman's telegram and was working for Old Man Payton.

It was the towheaded youth, Todd, who brought Clint the news of each man's arrival, and Clint gave the lad two bits for each piece of information.

"I could find out more, Clint," the boy offered, but Clint shook his head.

"We only needed to know when they arrived, Todd. You did fine."

The boy beamed at the compliment and went off to show the other children his wealth.

Nancy came out to the porch and stood next to Clint.

"Both men are here, then?" she asked.

"Yes."

"And will you and Ron . . . kill them?"

"Possibly."

"Because of me," she said flatly.

"Don't think that."

"What else should I think?" she asked. "Either you'll kill them or they'll kill you, and it will be because of me."

"For a man to die this way, Nancy, is his own choice. Nobody forces him to draw on another man. There's always another choice."

"Like what?"

"Like turning around and walking away."

"Do men like you and Ron Diamond do that, Clint? Do you walk away?"

"When it's necessary."

"Well, then, walk away. Now. I'm freeing you from any obligation you might feel toward me and the children."

"What makes you think I feel obligated?"

"Why else would you stay?"

"Maybe I just want to."

"And Ron?"

"You'll have to ask him that, Nancy. I can't answer for him."

"I can," she said. "He's staying because of Lisa, and you're staying because of—"

When she stopped Clint looked at her and asked, "Because of what?"

"Never mind. Dinner's ready. That's what I came out to tell you."

"All right," he said. "I'll be there in a minute."

"Find Ron and tell him, won't you? I think he's in the back with Lisa."

Clint walked around to the back of the house, wondering what it was Nancy thought was keeping him here. Or who it was. Did she think it was Belinda? If she did, she was wrong, and he meant to show her just how wrong.

Ron and Lisa were playing behind the house, and he sent Lisa in for dinner.

"What about Ron?"

"I'll be in with Clint in a minute, honey."

"You'll sit next to me," she shouted, running toward the house.

"Where else does she think I'd sit?" Diamond said to

Clint. He looked at the Gunsmith's face and said, "Hendry's here?"

"Yes."

"They're both there, then. Think they'll come right away?"

"They may not come at all."

"Well, maybe we can push them a little. I really can't afford to sit and wait for them to make a move."

"No, we can't afford that," Clint said. Diamond had to get on the move again, tracking the men who killed his wife and child. Clint's reason was simpler than that. If you let the other man make the first move where and when he chose, you gave him the upper hand.

No man ever lived very long giving the other man the upper hand.

But sometimes showdowns just never happen, for the worst situations just seem to resolve themselves.

TWENTY-ONE

Overnight several unexpected things occurred.

First, Kyle Webster returned home without warning and found his wife happily riding his foreman, her naked ass making loud slapping noises everytime she came down on the man.

Second, Kyle Webster took out a gun and shot his foreman, Ike Turner, dead. This particularly surprised Mrs. Webster who never thought her husband had it in him to do such a thing. She climbed off the dead foreman and faced her husband, fondling her breasts in front of him and aroused by the unexpected act of violence she'd just witnessed.

Which was nothing compared to the one she was about to witness.

For the third totally unexpected thing Kyle Webster did was fire his gun a second time, this time sending a bullet right into his wife, surprising the life right out of her.

Clint and Ron heard about this the following day as they rode into town. It was the number one topic of conversation on the street and in the saloon. It seemed that everyone but Kyle Webster had known about his wife and his foreman carrying on whenever he was out of town, and money had been bet on what would happen if the cuckolded husband ever returned unexpectedly.

Nobody collected. The number two topic of discussion was what should be done with the money that was in the kitty.

Webster, being the wronged husband, of course, got off scot-free, especially since the judge's wife had run off five years earlier with some eastern drummer, the judge swearing he'd kill them both if he ever laid eyes on them again.

As it turned out, Webster had no real interest in the piece of land the orphanage was sitting on, and Payton, hearing this, lost interest as well.

Payton fired Taylor Hendry who, being the professional that he was, took it in stride—along with a smaller portion of money than originally agreed on for his trouble.

Ted Willis, on the other hand, when fired by Kyle Webster, did not take kindly to it, and decided to take it out on either Clint Adams or Ron Diamond, whomever he should happen upon first.

So it came to be that Taylor Hendry, Ted Willis, Clint Adams, and Ron Diamond all happened to be in town at the same time two days after the double shooting, when everything had been settled for everyone . . . except Willis.

Clint and Diamond were in the saloon enjoying a couple of beers when Hendry entered and approached their table.

"Something we can do for you, Hendry?" Clint asked.

"If you'll pardon me, gentlemen, I felt that since I would not get to cross swords with either of you this trip, you might not be above allowing me to buy you a drink."

Clint looked at Diamond who said, "Why not?"

"Thank you," Hendry said. "It is seldom that I get to indulge in the company of two such celebrated individuals."

"We're flattered," Clint said.

No sooner had Hendry returned from the bar with three beers than Ted Willis entered the saloon and, spying the three of them, approached their table.

"I want one of you," Willis said, ignoring Hendry.

"I hope that doesn't include me, dear boy," Hendry said.

"I don't even know who you are, dude," Willis said, "so stay out of this."

"Rude chap," Hendry said into his beer, and he sat back to observe.

"One of us?" Clint asked.

"Either one, it don't matter to me."

"You can't be getting paid for this, kid," Diamond said.

"This is on my own, old man," Willis said. "Which one of you will it be?"

"What if both of us stand up?" Clint asked. "What would you do then?"

"Oh, jolly good question," Hendry said. "I can't wait to hear the answer to that one."

Willis seemed stunned by the question and actually took one step backward.

"You wouldn't," he said, finally finding his voice. "That wouldn't be fair."

"Who said life was fair, sonny?" Diamond asked in a nasty voice.

"You'd better take a walk, lad," Clint advised him.

The boy's face seemed on the verge of crumbling, and then he stiffened his chin and said, "No. Even if you both stand up and kill me, my name will live on as the man who faced you both!"

Clint stared at the young man with something akin to awe on his face, then turned to Diamond, and said, "Tell me he didn't actually say that."

"Oh, he said it, all right."

"I heard him as well," Hendry offered. "Utterly absurd thing to say!"

"Well, come on!" Willis demanded. "Let's get on with it."

"Christ," Clint said, "we can't get out of this one, can we?"

"It doesn't look like it," Diamond said.

"All right, kid," Clint said wearily, "just go and wait out in the street; one of us will be along in a minute."

"Don't get lonely," Diamond said.

"Only one of you?" Willis asked, and for a moment Clint thought the kid looked disappointed. Nah, must have been his imagination . . .

"One of us."

"Okay," Willis said, and he backed out of the saloon as if he expected to be shot in the back at any moment.

"Well, who's it going to be?" Diamond asked.

"I hate this," Clint said. "That kid ain't even dry behind the ears yet."

"If it will help you chaps out any, I could go out there for you," Hendry offered.

"Thanks, but no thanks," Clint told the Englishman.

"Just trying to be helpful."

"I'll go," Diamond said finally, after a few moments of silence had gone by.

"Why you?"

"Why not?"

"You're a little rusty."

"You said yourself he wasn't dry behind the ears yet."

"That doesn't mean he can't shoot."

"Well, one of us has to go."

"Why don't we just go out that back door?" Clint asked.

"You know the answer to that one."

If they walked away from this kid, the story would be told that they ran away, and they'd be fair game for any kid with a gun and a hankering for a reputation.

"Why don't you just flip a coin?" Hendry suggested.

"To see who gets to kill a kid?" Clint asked.

"If you don't," Hendry said, "that kid might die of old age waiting for one of you."

"He's got a point," Diamond said.

"All right, all right," Clint agreed, "we'll flip a coin."

"I'll do the honors," Hendry said, digging into his vest pocket. "Hope you don't mind if it's an English coin. It's my lucky piece."

He produced a foreign coin that neither Clint nor Diamond could identify and said, "Call the flip."

"Heads," Clint said, just a scant second before Diamond was about to say the same thing.

The coin went up, flipping end over end, paused just shy of the ceiling, then fell back down, still flipping, and landed in Hendry's right hand. He proceeded to slap his hand over the back of his left hand and then took it away so they could see the coin.

"Damn foreign coin," Diamond muttered, unable to tell heads from tails.

"What is it?" Clint asked.

"I'm afraid it's tails, my friends," Hendry said. "Mr. Diamond will do the honors."

Scowling, Diamond said, "Maybe I can wing him."

"Don't even think about it," Clint warned him. "He aims to kill you, Ron."

"Yeah, you're right," Diamond said. "You gonna watch?"

"Hell, no," Clint said. "I'll have another beer while waiting for you."

Hendry looked torn between two possible decisions. He wanted to watch, but did not want to lose face in front of Clint by doing so.

"Oh, bloody hell," he said, standing up. "I've got to watch this."

"Watch it, then."

Hendry went out behind Diamond, and Clint ordered fresh beers. After a few moments, there was a single shot.

When the two men re-entered, Hendry was shaking his head.

"The lad never got his hand on his gun," the Englishman said.

As Diamond sat down, looking morose, Clint said, "Drink your beer before it gets cold. The sheriff should be here any minute."

TWENTY-TWO

Clint and Diamond spent one last night at the orphanage.

Taylor Hendry had proved handy to have around because he was the witness who kept the sheriff from locking Diamond up again.

Afterward they returned to the orphanage, and it was then that Nancy Sharpe told them that both Webster and Payton had officially withdrawn their offers for the land.

"We'll be leaving in the morning," Clint told Nancy, and she had simply lowered her head and said, "Yes."

In his room that night, Clint briefly considered going down the hall to Nancy Sharpe's room, but finally decided against it and tried to get to sleep in spite of the fact that his aroused condition was making it difficult. He just knew that if Belinda made a visit to him tonight, he'd let her in.

Sure enough, just as he was dozing off, he became aware of someone trying his door and, finding it locked, knocking gently.

He rose, naked, and padded to the door, unlocking it. She slipped inside and he knew from the fragrance of her hair and her body that it wasn't Belinda.

It was Nancy.

She stared at him after he closed the door and turned, frankly inspecting his nude form and finally bringing her eyes to rest on his rigid manhood.

"Who were you expecting?" she asked.

"Uh, Nancy—"

"No, don't bother, Clint," she said. "I know Belinda came to you one night."

"You do?"

"I saw her, and I know she stayed with you for a while. I don't blame you; she's a lovely child."

"Nancy—"

"I also know that you never let her in again after that night. Why?"

"Because she wasn't you," he said before he realized he was going to say it.

She smiled and said, "I was hoping you would say something like that."

She opened her robe then and let it fall to the floor, revealing herself to be naked beneath it. Her body was much fuller and more mature than Belinda's, and Clint's eyes devoured her. Her breasts were large, round, and firm with rigid, dark nipples. Her belly was convex rather than concave, her hips wide, her thighs fleshy. Between her thighs he wanted to delve with his tongue.

"I won't have to threaten to wake the whole house, will I?" she asked.

"No, Nancy," he said, moving toward her, "you won't have to do that . . ."

In the morning as Clint and Diamond were readying to leave, Nancy thanked them for all they had done.

"We didn't do that much, Nancy," Clint said.

"You did enough," she assured both of them. "You were here, and you were prepared to risk your lives. Had it not been for Lucille Webster's unfaithfulness . . . I guess we have that woman to thank, after all."

"Now that the land is secure, how will you keep the

orphanage going without money from the east?'' Clint asked her.

"I'll write some letters and see if we can't get some support, but even if we don't, we'll manage.''

"If I come back this way . . .'' Clint said lamely.

"Of course.''

Off to one side, Ron Diamond was saying good-bye to little Lisa.

"Why can't you stay, Ron?''

"I have something I have to do, honey.''

"Will you come back?''

"I don't know.''

At that point she grabbed him around the legs and hugged him, crying, "Please come back, Ron. Please come back.''

He picked her up in his arms to hug her and said, "If I can, honey, if I can.''

Nancy, seeing that Diamond might have some difficulty with Lisa, took the little girl from his arms.

"Take care of each other,'' she told the two men.

"You take care of these kids, ma'am,'' Diamond said.

"I will.''

"We will,'' Belinda said, moving next to Nancy.

"Yes,'' Nancy said, putting one arm around the younger woman's waist, "we will.''

Clint and Diamond mounted and, with a wave, rode off away from Duneden and away from the orphanage.

About a mile later, Clint pulled to a stop and said to Diamond, "Ron, why don't you just go back there and get that little girl.''

"Adams, I asked you to keep me from doing something stupid, not encourage me.''

"That's what I'm trying to do, Ron,'' Clint said.

"I've got something that needs doing, Clint, before I can think about anything else. Are you coming?''

"Yeah, I'm coming."

As they rode, Diamond said, "Damned stupid thing staying in that town so long, anyway. Probably never pick up their trail again."

Giving up the hope that he could talk Diamond out of continuing his search, Clint said, "Yes, Ron, we will."

"How?"

"They're in Montana."

"What? How do you know that?"

"When I sent the telegram to Rick in Texas, I asked him to check around for us," Clint explained. "I told him we were looking for two men riding together, one with a wounded shoulder, the other with a facial scar."

"And he found them?"

"He thinks he's got them spotted in Montana where they met up with another group of men."

"How many?"

"Four or five."

"So if it's them, there's six or seven of them now, at least."

"That's the way it looks," Clint said, "if Rick's information is right."

"And it usually is?"

"Almost always."

Diamond thought it over a moment and then asked Clint, "Does that change your mind?"

"Does it change yours?"

"Hell, no!"

"Well, then," Clint said, "I guess I can be just about as stubborn as you can."

A mile farther on, they saw a familiar figure waiting for them. He was clad in dark clothing with black gloves on each hand and sitting astride a glossy, black colt. The animal was so black he glistened as if his coat were wet.

"That's quite a horse," Clint said to Taylor Hendry.

"You should talk," Hendry said, eyeing Duke with frank appreciation.

"He looks young."

"He's three," Hendry said, patting his horse's neck with obvious affection. "Yours?"

"Duke's a little long in the tooth now," Clint said, showing similar affection for the big black gelding. "He's nearly seven or so. He was supposed to have been a yearling when I got him, but he was so big that I couldn't be sure. He might be eight or even as old as nine. Still, I figure seven."

"He's still a beauty."

Strictly speaking, Clint admitted that for sheer beauty Duke did not match the other, but for stature he was more than the younger horse's match.

"You name your horse, too?" Diamond asked.

"Sure," Hendry said. "Satan."

"Why?"

"Because he's as black as death must be, and when I die, I'll surely see Satan himself."

"Why name him at all?" Diamond asked. "I never had a horse long enough to name it."

"Then that explains why you have to ask," Clint said. Turning his attention back to Hendry, he asked, "Where are you headed?"

"Nowhere in particular," the young gunman said with a shrug. "I did have a thought that perhaps I might tag along with you fellas."

"It's not going to be a picnic where we're going," Diamond warned.

"If that's the case, it sounds like you might be in need of an extra gun."

"It's possible," Clint agreed. "It's also possible you might learn something."

Hendry grinned at that and said, "Granted."

"Tell me," Clint said, "what happens along the way if someone decides to hire you to make a try for one of us?"

Hendry shrugged and said, "Well, a man's got to make a living, doesn't he?"

Clint looked at Diamond, then nodded at Hendry, and said, "As long as we understand each other."

Hendry grinned and said, "I highly doubt that, old chap, but I guess we three are nearer to understanding each other than anyone else would be."

Clint doubted that, but kept silent.

"Let's stop talking then," Diamond said, "and get on with it."

Hendry wheeled his horse about and they all rode north, three abreast.

TWENTY-THREE

Eight days later they entered the town of Hell's Crossing, Montana, the last location that Rick Hartman's informants had spotted the two men whom Clint and Ron were searching for. Of course, it was in this town that the two men had joined up with the four or five others, and it was unknown as to whether this meeting had been planned or was spur of the moment.

The bitter cold made its way to Clint's bones, as if it instinctively knew that the Gunsmith hated cold weather.

"I hate cold weather," Clint said as they approached the livery.

"Don't think about it," Taylor Hendry suggested.

"Easier said than done."

"At least it's not snowing," Ron Diamond said.

"Yet," Clint said, looking up at the sky doubtfully.

They turned their horses over to the liveryman and once again Ron Diamond had to stand by and listen as the man admired both Duke and Satan. He promised to take excellent care of both animals.

"Take good care of mine, too," Diamond said, handing the man the reins.

"Uh, yes, sir, real good care," the man said.

"You've got to get yourself a better horse, Diamond," Hendry commented as they headed for a saloon or hotel, whichever came first.

"I won't need one after this," Diamond said and Clint looked uninformed as Hendry looked to him, puzzled by the remark. In fact, the Gunsmith was uninformed as to Diamond's plans after the hunt was over. Hell, he wasn't even sure what Diamond was planning when they finally caught up to the men. The man just never talked about it.

They came to a hotel first and it was decided that Clint would go in and get three rooms—or as many as were available—drop off all three sets of saddlebags, and then meet Diamond and Hendry at the nearest saloon.

In the hotel lobby, Clint found himself thinking back to other men he had traveled with. In the past he had often found himself in the company of men who lived by their guns—as did he, like it or not.

He'd ridden with Bat Masterson and Wyatt Earp. The three of them had gotten along very well and had become fast friends.

He'd worked with both Bat Masterson and Bill Tilghman in Dodge City, which had been an experience, but not an altogether unpleasant one.

He'd ridden with the likes of Fred Hammer, the only black gunman he'd ever known, and Dan Chow, one of two Oriental gunmen he'd met. Although he'd hesitate to call either of them his friends, they'd worked together pretty well.

He wondered how this particular trio would end up.

He obtained two rooms for the three of them, dropped all the saddlebags off in the same room—they'd decide on the sleeping arangements later—and then headed for the saloon. He figured a cold beer wouldn't be a problem, but he was also looking forward to a pot of strong, black, hot coffee.

Outside of Hell's Crossing was a log cabin and inside it a fire was burning. There were five men in the cabin enjoying the warmth of the fire, and two of them were Lincoln Gilmartin and Sam Henderson.

The other three men were Dave Burke, Steve Perry, and Bob Killerman. Gilmartin and Henderson had met these three—plus Dan Adams and Doc Lewis—in Hell's Crossing and had signed on to hit the town's bank.

There were two catches, though.

Number one was that they were waiting for two more men whom Adams and Lewis had since gone to meet.

The other was that they had to wait until the payrolls for the two logging companies in the area were in the bank, which wouldn't be until the fifteenth of the month. It was now the twelfth and Gilmartin and Henderson had been in Hell's Crossing for nearly two weeks.

Doc Lewis, the leader of the group, had asked them, "You ain't on the run, are you?"

"Hell, no," Gilmartin had replied.

"We don't need anybody who's on the run," Lewis had said. "I've planned this very carefully."

"I told you we ain't," Gilmartin insisted, and Lewis had accepted his word—possibly because he needed more men to round the job out.

Later, Henderson had asked, "What if there's somebody still looking for us for that New Mexico thing, Linc?"

"Well, there ain't."

"If there is and these guys find out, they'll kill us."

"Do you want to turn down a piece of this job they're offering us, Sam?"

"No, but I think—"

"Just let me do the thinking and the talking, all right?"

"Sure, Linc," Henderson had replied doubtfully, "sure."

Now Linc Gilmartin could see that Sam Henderson was starting to get jumpy after being cooped up in that cabin.

"Sam, why don't you go out and get more wood for the fire?"

Without a word Henderson got up and went outside to do what he was told.

"What's he so nervous about?" Dave Burke asked.

"I don't know."

"You guys wouldn't have lied to Doc about being on the run, would you?"

Gilmartin looked at Burke, who was physically the biggest man in the cabin. In fact, when he stood up he seemed to fill the cabin. He was just above six feet tall and well over three hundred pounds, and a more fearsome man you'd never want to meet.

"Well, to tell you the truth," Gilmartin said, "I know for a fact that I ain't on the run, but I can't be as sure about Henderson, you know?"

"Well, if we find out that he is," Burke said, "I know what Doc'll do."

"What?" Gilmartin asked.

Burke smiled and, if it was possible, suddenly seemed uglier.

"He'll give him to me."

Gilmartin shivered as Burke once again directed his attention to the fire. Linc was glad he had decided to set Henderson up because he was suddenly sure that he was going to have to throw these fellas something—or someone—and it sure as hell wasn't going to be him.

TWENTY-FOUR

Clint found Diamond and Hendry in a small saloon that seemed to be filled with loggers. Hell's Crossing was a logging town, built specifically for the needs of the loggers working the area. When the logging operations broke up, the town would die. The buildings would rot, some would fall, but some would remain standing, simply to mark the spot where once there was a small but thriving town, where once there was money to be made.

Loggers, he knew from experience, liked to fight when they were relaxing. He hoped they hadn't chosen the wrong saloon, but it was the nearest to the hotel, and, therefore, the easiest to meet at.

He got himself a beer from the bar and joined the others at their table. He positioned his chair so that he could see the entire room.

"Noisy, isn't it?" Hendry asked.

"Loggers," Clint said. "They're a noisy bunch."

"Let's finish these and find a quieter place," Diamond said. "I can't hear myself think."

"I can't argue with that," Clint said.

They finished their drinks in silence, rather than fight to be heard over the din, but as they turned to leave one big logger seemed to take offense.

"Oh, ho," the big man shouted, "seems these strangers don't like drinking in the company of loggers."

The man stood almost as big as a ponderosa pine, and he had a huge, remarkably clean black beard which covered a massive chest.

"You fellas don't like loggers?" he demanded as the place suddenly fell silent.

"Noise," Taylor Hendry said, "we don't like noise."

"Oh, we're too noisy!" the man shouted. "You hear that, lads? This here fella with the funny accent says we're too noisy."

Suddenly, every man in the place shouted at once, nearly lifting the roof off the place.

"That noisy enough for you, laddie?" the big man asked.

Clint could see in Taylor Hendry's eyes that he was going to do something foolish, but he was too slow to stop him. Hendry smashed one gloved hand into the center of the big man's face, landing the blow square on the man's nose. Blood streamed from the man's nostrils, falling onto his mustache and beard, but the man merely grinned, allowing the blood to stain his teeth as well.

"Mmmm," he said, licking blood off his teeth. "Think the taste of my own blood bothers me, lad?"

A massive fist crashed into Hendry's face and the young gunman was lifted off his feet by the blow.

"Shit!" Clint snapped, and at the same time he and Diamond drove fists into the big man's gut. Neither did much damage, though, as the man simply grunted and grinned at them.

"Not good enough, lads," he said. He put one hand against each's chest and pushed, lifting them off their feet and depositing them on the floor with Hendry between them.

"Jesus," Hendry said, licking blood from his bottom lip.

"Think we can make the door?" Diamond asked.

"Not in one piece," Clint said.

"Shall we put a hole in him?" Hendry asked.

"I don't think we've got enough bullets," Clint said with a touch of humor.

"Well, what will it be, lads?" the big man asked. "Would you rather fight or drink?"

"I'd rather drink," Clint replied and then looked at his two companions and said, "What about you, fellas?"

"A drink sounds good," Diamond said.

"Definitely," Hendry agreed.

"Hey, boys!" the big man shouted. "We got us some sports, here. Nary a one of them went for his gun—not that it would have done them any good." The man looked down at them and said, "Come on, then, lads. Up on your feet and to the bar. The drinks are on McCoy."

There was a stampede to the bar as Clint, Diamond, and Hendry climbed to their feet.

"You all right?" Clint asked Hendry.

"Fine," the Englishman said. "I don't think he hit me as hard as he could have, or I'd be dead."

"I guess he's McCoy," Diamond said.

"I guess we'd better have that drink," Clint said. "I think Mr. McCoy would be a much better friend than enemy."

"Can't argue that," Diamond said as they moved to join the crowd at the bar.

They spent most of the evening in the saloon called The Logger's Saloon drinking with McCoy, who seemed to be able to consume more liquor and beer than the three of them put together. In addition, he drank his beer from a bucket. They met McCoy's coworkers, and they met the woman who worked in the saloon, a Irish lass named Rachel.

"Rachel, me lass," McCoy said to the plump, auburn-haired woman who was firmly entrenched on his lap, "how would you like to spend the night with one of my new friends?''

Rachel, who was really more than a lass—thirty-five if she was a day, but still prime—looked over the three of them and couldn't seem to make up her mind which one interested her most.

"I guess that's up to them, McCoy," she said, kissing him on his battered nose and wiggling her butt in his lap.

"What do you say, lads?"

Looking hopeful, Hendry looked over at his two comrades and said, "What do you say, chaps?"

"No, thanks," said Diamond and then hastily added to McCoy and Rachel, "no offense meant."

"None taken," McCoy said. "How about you, friend?" he asked, looking at Clint.

"I think I'll pass, McCoy," Clint said. "Let the youngster here have a chance."

"Ah, she'd kill him," McCoy said, looking at Hendry with a grin.

"I'll take my chances," Hendry said. He was studying the woman's sturdy calves, which were exposed because her skirt had ridden all the way up her thighs. A glance a little higher told the three of them that she was wearing no underwear at all.

"What do you say, girl?" he asked.

She studied Hendry for a few silent moments and then asked, "Will you take off them gloves?"

"Only for you, lovely lady."

"I like the way he talks, McCoy," she said then. "He talks even nicer than you."

"Oh, ho, she likes your accent, boy," McCoy said. "Here, I've got her all ready for you. Take her." With that, McCoy lifted Rachel and literally tossed her to Hendry. The young gunman tried to catch her, but the chair flipped over backward under the pressure, and they both ended up on the floor.

"Come on," Rachel said eagerly, getting to her feet, "I'm hotter than a rooster in July."

Hendry got to his feet and said to his companions, "See you chaps in the morning."

"Enjoy," Clint said.

McCoy said, "It ain't generally known, lads, but there's more gals in the back room, waiting to be had—for a price, of course."

"I don't usually pay for it, McCoy," Clint said. "I'll still pass."

"Ha! A man of principle. I knew it as soon as I saw you. And what about you?"

"I've got just as many principles as Clint," Diamond said. "Right now I'd rather have another drink."

A while later Clint decided that maybe McCoy was drunk enough to field a question. He described the two men they were looking for and asked McCoy if he remembered seeing them.

"I can't say as I have," McCoy replied, "but I can ask around—if there's good reason."

Clint looked at Diamond because it was up to him to handle that one.

"There's good reason, McCoy."

"Such as?"

Diamond hesitated.

"If I'm gonna start using my friends as informers, my new friend, I'll have to know why."

After a moment Diamond said, "They raped and killed my wife. She was carrying our first child."

McCoy suddenly became somber and apparently sober, and Clint could have sworn he saw tears glistening in the big man's eyes.

"That's a good enough reason, friend," McCoy said. "I'm sorry for your loss, and I'll do whatever I can to help you find the rats that did it, rest assured."

"I'm going to the hotel," Diamond said then, standing up. "I'd appreciate any help you can give us, McCoy."

"Say no more."

"We'll bunk together, Ron," Clint said. "Hendry's a little occupied."

Diamond nodded and left the saloon.

"That man's carrying around a lot of pain," McCoy said.

"Yes, he is."

"And you and your other friend are trying to help him?"

"We're doing our best."

"Friend," McCoy said, slapping Clint hard on the shoulder, "let's have a drink to friends helping friends."

"Mr. McCoy," Clint said, moving his shoulder to make sure it wasn't broken, "this time I'll buy."

When Clint got back to the hotel, Ron Diamond was sitting by the window. From the room next door they could hear a bed squeaking, and two different voices crying out alternately.

"Sounds like they're killing each other," Clint commented.

"It's been going on like that since I got back."

"Oh, to be young again."

"We moving out in the morning?"

"I think we should give McCoy time to find out something for us," Clint said. "That big bear is bound and determined to help you find those fellas."

"All right," Diamond said. "We'll give him a day. What about your friend, Hartman?"

"If this town has a telegraph, I'll send a wire. If not, we'll have to wait until we get to the next town."

"Fair enough."

"Can't get to sleep?"

Diamond shook his head.

"Thinking about Delores isn't going to help, Ron."

"That's what I'm feeling guilty about, Clint."

"What?"

"I haven't been thinking about Delores."

"Lisa?"

Diamond nodded.

"She's a sweet little girl, Ron."

"I know it," Diamond said, clenching both hands into fists, "but I can't go back there until I've done what I have to do."

"We haven't talked much about just what it is you intend to do when we find them, Ron."

"That's easy," Diamond said. "I'm going to kill them."

Clint started to say something, but then held it back. He understood the cold rage that was festering inside Ron Diamond. He'd felt it when Joanna Morgan was killed. There was no way a man could be talked out of a rage like that. It either had to burn itself out or be quenched. His own had been quenched by killing the man who had killed the woman he loved, and he wasn't proud of it. He hoped that Diamond's would burn itself out before the same thing happened.

"Well," Clint said, "I'm pretty drunk, so I'm going to turn in."

"I will, too," Diamond said, "soon."

Clint left Diamond alone with his thoughts and lowered himself into one of the beds. That was the last thing he remembered.

TWENTY-FIVE

Clint had never gotten the pot of coffee he'd wanted the night before, so over breakfast he had two, while Diamond and Hendry shared one.

"Hope me and Rachel didn't keep you chaps up last night," Hendry said, apologizing with a big grin on his face. "That lady certainly has a lot of energy."

"Didn't keep me up," Clint assured him.

"I had no problem," Diamond said.

"What are the plans for today?"

"I'm going to check the town out and see if they have a telegraph set up. Since there are logging operations in the area, I imagine that there is."

"And then?"

"We have to wait until we hear from McCoy."

"Then we'll be here at least a day?"

"At least," Clint said. "That gives you time to get reacquainted with Rachel, eh?"

"Plenty of time, my friend."

"Well," Clint said, "that's one way of keeping warm in this climate."

"The best way."

The day passed in an uneventful manner.

Clint sent another telegram to Rick in Labyrinth, Texas, but the reply was that he had no further information. He seemed to have lost track of the two men after Hell's Crossing.

All three men circulated through the small town, keeping their eyes and ears open, and when they met for dinner in a small café filled with loggers, they compared notes.

"Nothing," Hendry said.

"Nothing," Diamond said.

"That's what I got."

"What about your friend, Hartman?" Diamond asked.

"He's got nothing further."

"Nothing after this town?"

"Right."

"That means they've gone to ground somewhere."

"Maybe."

"What other explanation do you have?"

"They're still here."

"In Hell's Crossing?"

Clint nodded.

"So then they've gone to ground here," Hendry said, "and they're keeping out of sight. Why?"

"That remains to be seen," Clint said, "but we can do one of two things. We can keep on going, trying to pick up a trail that doesn't exist or we can wait here."

"For what?"

"For them to make a move."

"Like what?"

Clint shrugged and said, "Who knows? We have to wait and see."

Diamond frowned and said, "Who knows? We have to wait and see."

Diamond frowned and said, "I don't like staying in one spot too long. We did that already and look where it got us."

"Thanks a lot," Hendry said, alluding to the fact that by

staying in one spot they had met him and allowed him to join them. Both Clint and Diamond ignored the remark.

"Let's put off making a decision until we talk to McCoy later."

"You really think he's going to have anything?" Diamond said. "He was so drunk last night I doubt he'll even remember us."

"He'll remember," Clint said as the waitress brought their food. He watched her with interest as she set down their plates. He'd hid it quite well the night before, but Rachel had aroused him, and he needed someone to release the pent-up feelings.

"Thank you," he said when she'd finished.

"Oh, a polite one," she said, smiling. "Let me know if you need anything else."

"A couple of pots of coffee after this."

"I'll get them ready."

He watched her walk back to the kitchen, admiring the well-toned body. Some waitresses were thin, some plump; but usually they were all in fine condition. Solid hips, thighs, and calves, and the full breasts on this one aroused his interest even more. Her face was less than beautiful, but again she had fine features highlighted by a strong, straight nose and firm jaw. She had to be nearing forty, but he didn't mind that, either. On the way back to the kitchen, she gracefully eluded the grasp of two loggers, laughing with them.

"All right, then," Diamond said, oblivious to the object of Clint's attention, "let's eat and get over to the saloon and see if your big friend has a good memory."

"Fine," Clint said and began eating. As he had expected to find in a logging town, the food was very good. He hoped the coffee was good also.

●　　　●　　　●

After dinner Clint paid the bill and left something extra for the waitress, who graced him with another warm smile.

"Come back again," she said.

"Real soon," he assured her.

From the café, they went to the saloon. It was full of loggers, as was probably always the case, but had McCoy been there they would have had no problem spotting him.

"He's got such a good memory he can't even remember where the saloon is," Diamond muttered. "Maybe he's doing his drinking somewhere else tonight."

"That may be," Clint said, "but he'll be back here sooner or later. All we have to do is wait."

"Excuse me, chaps," Hendry said, "I see an old friend."

Clint looked across the room and saw Rachel sitting in a logger's lap.

"Just remember," Clint called out a warning to him, "she's a working girl."

Hendry waved a gloved hand and began making his way through the crowd.

Clint and Diamond stood at the bar, each with a beer, waiting for a table to open up.

"If they were here," Diamond said at one point "they'd stand out like sheep in a cow herd. They're not loggers."

"They're keeping low, Ron."

"Why?"

"Only one thing I can figure."

"Keep me in suspense."

"There's no stores here worth holding up, but there is a bank."

"What are they waiting for, then? Why haven't they hit it yet?"

"My guess is they ran across some fellas who needed some extra guns for the job."

"That still doesn't say why they haven't already hit it."

"It's only the thirteenth of the month."

"So?"

"The payroll for the logging companies will be here on the fifteenth."

"And they're waiting for it," Diamond said, understanding at last.

"We've got two more days, Ron."

"If they intend to hit the bank at all," Diamond said. "If not, then we waste two more days."

"Don't be a pessimist," Clint said. "Let's at least hear what McCoy has to say."

"Speak of the devil . . ."

Clint looked at the doorway and saw McCoy filling it. The big man saw them immediately.

"My friends," McCoy shouted, approaching them with outstretched arms. He gave them each a squeeze on the shoulder and then ordered a bucket of beer.

"Come on, we'll get a table," he said when he had his bucket.

"There aren't any—" Clint began, but he realized that he should have known better.

McCoy moved toward a table and with one swipe of his free hand and arm cleared it. The three loggers who had been sitting at it simply picked themselves off the floor and made for the bar.

"Pull up a chair," McCoy invited them, seating himself. "Where's your other friend?"

"Negotiating," Clint said.

McCoy looked across the room and saw Hendry talking earnestly with Rachel, who was still seated in a logger's lap.

"Don't worry," McCoy said, "your friend will outbid Dennehy."

"Never mind that," Diamond said. "What did you find out for us."

"Oh, yeah, I was supposed to find out some things for you, wasn't I?"

Diamond gave Clint an I-told-you-so look while McCoy took a huge swig of beer from his bucket. He'd had a few already before this one; that was obvious. He got as much on his shirt front as he did in his mouth.

"Well, boys, your information was good," the big logger said, wiping his mouth with his sleeve.

"What do you mean?" Diamond demanded.

"Two men fitting your description were here, and for all I can find out they still might be."

"When did they get here?"

"About two weeks ago."

"Damn!" Diamond said. "They're long gone by now."

"Not necessarily," McCoy said. "See, they was seen riding in, but they wasn't seen riding out."

"So? They could have ridden out at night."

"Your friend here doesn't think so."

Diamond looked at Clint who said, "No, I don't. How many logging companies are working this region, McCoy?"

"Two."

"And when do the payrolls come in?"

"Both on the fifteenth." He put his bucket down on the table and leaned forward. "Shit, you think they're gonna hit our payrolls?"

"Any other strangers come into town during these past two weeks?"

"There's always strangers riding through."

"Got any law in this town?"

"Not official. My boss, Cal Rifkin, he appointed a sheriff to keep things quiet."

"Maybe we should talk to the law."

"Why not?" McCoy said. "I can get you in to see him because he's my brother."

"Tonight?"

"Tomorrow's only the fourteenth," McCoy said. "Ain't that soon enough."

"Will he listen?"

"He'll listen to me," the big man said with assurance. "He's my little brother."

Clint looked at Diamond and said, "What do you say?"

"We just wait for them to hit the bank, huh?"

"We get what you want, and we save these people's payrolls."

"If they show up."

Clint nodded and said, "That's right, Ron. If they show up."

"Hell," Diamond said after a moment, "why not? Nothing else has gone right; maybe this will."

"Damn!" McCoy said, slamming his fist on the table, almost splintering it. "Let's have a drink on it."

"I've got a previous engagement, McCoy," Clint said, standing up.

"Found yourself a female you don't have to pay for, huh?"

"Maybe. Keep my friend here company, will you?"

"You bet."

Diamond looked at Clint and said, "Thanks a lot" sarcastically.

As he was leaving, Clint heard McCoy saying, "I'm gonna introduce you to all of my friends, lad. There's got to be one you'll like for yourself."

TWENTY-SIX

The door to the cabin slammed inward and Sam Henderson reached for his gun.

"Easy," Linc Gilmartin said, putting his hand on his partner's arm. "You'll make these fellas think you're afraid of something."

Henderson eased his hand away from his gun as Doc Lewis entered, followed closely by Dan Adams and two other men.

"You're late," Steve Perry said.

"So?" Lewis replied. It was obvious that he was in a foul mood.

"I was just saying—"

"Well, don't. Any coffee on?"

Burke roused himself and said, "It's on, and it's hot. Welcome back, Doc. Wanna introduce your friends?"

"This is Earl Hansen," Lewis said, pointing to a man who couldn't have been more than five feet five, "and this here's Christopher Cord."

Everyone in the room reacted to the second man's name in their own way. Perry and Killerman stared; Burke's mouth spread in a satisfied grin; Henderson frowned concernedly; and Linc Gilmartin rubbed his jaw and sized the man up.

"You know who he is?" Henderson said in a low tone.

"Of course, I do," Gilmartin replied. "He's got a big rep.

They call him the Rattler because he's supposed to be so fast.''

"Well, don't get any ideas," Henderson said. "I didn't sign on to face Chris Cord.''

"He's on our side, Sam," Gilmartin said, "remember?''

"Sure," Henderson said, "just so long as you remember.''

"Get yourselves some coffee, boys," Doc Lewis said to the newcomers. "You can get introduced later.''

Gilmartin watched the man known as the Rattler as he crossed the room to the fireplace. He was tall and muscled, had a flat-cheeked face with a heavy mustache, and wore a Colt on his hip. He seemed totally unconcerned about the other men in the room as he poured himself a cup of coffee.

"Burke," Doc Lewis called, and Burke went into a corner of the room with Lewis and Dan Adams.

"They might be talking about us," Henderson whispered.

"If you don't get hold of your nerves, you're gonna get us both killed," Gilmartin hissed. "Now, relax. I got some thinking to do.''

His thinking revolved around the fact that with Chris Cord around, it might be harder for him and Henderson to take the money away from these jaspers after the job was done. He might just have to settle for a cut. That would mean throwing them Henderson in order to make sure he got a bigger cut. A nine-way split was way too big, even for the amount of money Doc Lewis had been talking about.

In his mind, Gilmartin was settling for nothing less than an eighth—and maybe less, if he could work it out.

Clint met the waitress coming out of the café. She was bent over, locking the door. When she turned, she bumped right into him and he liked the way her breasts felt.

"Hi," he said, "you said come back anytime."

She looked at him for a moment before recognizing him. "So I did," she said, "but as you can see, I'm closing for the night."

"You own the café?"

"I own it, but I can't cook worth a damn, which is why I wait tables."

They stood facing each other for a few moments, only an inch between them. "I don't imagine a woman has a problem with loneliness in a town like this."

"Some women don't," she said. "There are sure a lot of men to go around, but some women are particular about who they fall into bed with. That's what we're talking about, ain't it? Going to bed?"

"I guess that's what we're talking about."

"You figure I can give you something those girls at the saloon can't?"

"Maybe I just want a woman to go to bed with me because she wants to and not because she's being paid to."

"Don't like paying for it, eh?"

"No."

"Makes you kind of unusual," she said. "Most men don't care how they come by it as long as they come by it."

"Guess I'm unusual."

"Are you unusual in any other ways?"

"That's something you'll have to find out . . . if you're curious enough."

"Why don't you walk me to my room," she suggested, "and I'll see how much curiosity I can work up."

"Fine."

By the time they arrived at her door, she'd worked up a fair amount of curiosity and drew him inside with her. They undressed hurriedly and each seemed to want it as badly as the other.

"Just put it in me this time," she said huskily, "and we'll go slow next time."

He lowered her to the bed and mounted her like a rutting bull and they proceeded to seek their own satisfaction with little or no thought for each other. It was not the way Clint usually spent his time with a woman, but he found that he'd been wanting it even more than he'd thought. Since she felt the same way, there were no complaints—except from the bed, which sounded as if it wanted to collapse.

"All right, now that we're all here, let's get down to it," Doc Lewis said, taking center stage in the middle of the room by standing at the room's only table.

"Mind if I ask a question or two first?" Chris Cord asked.

"Go ahead."

"I don't know how much you've told the others, but you haven't told me anything about this job, except that there's a lot of money in it," Cord said. "Now, some of these fellas—you, Adams, Burke—I know, but the others I don't. Why do we need nine men for this job?"

"That's an easy question, Cord," Lewis said. "We need nine men because the money we're after isn't in one bank, it's in two."

"We're gonna take two banks?" Sam Henderson said in disbelief.

"That's right," Lewis said, looking at Henderson and then at all the others. "We'll go in four and four, with one man outside holding all the horses. I'm pretty sure that'll be you, Henderson."

Henderson didn't look happy about that. He'd be the only man standing in the street while the bank robberies were going on.

"We're gonna work it out so that we go in and come out at the same time."

"Where are the two banks?" Linc Gilmartin asked. "This won't work if they're at opposite ends of the town." He remembered seeing one bank while he was in town, but not the other.

"Good question," Lewis said approvingly. "They're across the street from each other, which is exactly why it will work.

"When are we doing this?" Chris Cord asked.

Lewis said, "On the fifteenth. The money will get here in the morning, but the men aren't paid until three o'clock. We'll hit them in between those times."

"This is gonna go off like clockwork with only one day to work on it?" Cord said.

"If everybody does his part, there'll be no problem," Doc Lewis said. "More questions?" There weren't any. "Anybody want out?"

Nobody did. "All right. Gather 'round this table and take a look at the plans."

Later, after they'd gone slower and he'd shown her how he could care for her pleasure as much as his own, she said, "Well, you are unusual, aren't you?"

"I just wanted to make sure you enjoyed it as much as I did."

"There aren't too many men like you around."

"Is that why it's been so long for you between men?"

"I told you," she said, winding his hair around her finger. "I'm particular about who I bed down with."

"Well, I'm glad I got your curiosity up."

"So am I," she said, rolling over to press herself against him. He gripped her hips and pulled her over so that she was lying on top of him. She propped herself up so that her breasts dangled in his face, and he began to suck them alternately, rolling the nipples around with his tongue and squeezing her breasts with his hands.

"Mmmm," she moaned, deep in her throat, and then she said, "You know, there's still something I'm curious about. Do you mind?"

"Be my guest."

She wriggled down until she was nestled comfortably between his legs, satisfying her curiosity in a particularly satisfying way.

After he'd gone over the plans several times, Doc Lewis went outside and left the men to study the floor plans of the two banks. As he'd expected, Chris Cord followed him out.

"What's my part supposed to be, Doc?" Cord asked. "You didn't include me in no bank jobs just to watch the tellers and customers."

"Like you said inside, Cord," Lewis said. "Some of us you know—me, Dan Adams, and Burke. With you, that makes four, and a four-way split is a lot better than one with nine." Lewis looked at Cord and said, "Understand?"

"I understand, Doc," Christopher Cord said, laying his right hand on his gun, "I understand real well."

Still later, it was Clint who settled between her legs and satisfied his curiosity. He slid his hands beneath her to cup her buttocks while he sucked and licked her, and she gripped the back of her head and raised her hips to meet the pressure of his mouth.

"Ooh, God, that's it, right there, suck me there . . ." she moaned, pressing his face tightly against her.

He sucked her there and suddenly she was bucking and writhing beneath him. Before her orgasm could fade, he mounted her and drove himself into her, bringing her to a second climax before the first was over. As she reached her peak, he joined her, emptying himself into her in long, almost painful spurts.

"You know," she said just seconds later and still breathless, "we really should exchange names."

TWENTY-SEVEN

As it turned out, McCoy's first name was Errol—"But don't ever call me that!"—and his brother, the unofficial lawman, was named Sean.

Sean McCoy listened to what Clint had to say, while his brother and Ron Diamond simply stood off to one side, content to let the Gunsmith be the spokesman.

"If what you say is true," Sean McCoy said when Clint finished his story, "then we've got to figure out which bank they're going to hit."

"Why not both?" Clint asked.

"It can't be done."

"Why not? On the way over here I noticed that the banks are right across the street from each other. Our information says that there are at least six or seven men. With a couple more they might be able to rob both banks and get away with it."

"Not if we're waiting for them," Sean McCoy said. He turned to his brother and said, "Can you get me some good men?"

"I can get you good men," McCoy said, "but they ain't necessarily going to be good with a gun."

"That's all right," Sean McCoy said, "I ain't all that handy myself, but if we get enough men shooting, maybe they'll hit somebody."

"Diamond and I will split up," Clint said, "one with each group. That might help."

"We appreciate this," Sean said. "That is, if it really happens and we stop them. Big brother, we'll have to see if we can't get us some men. Since both payrolls might be in danger, I'm sure people will cooperate."

"Right you are, brother. I'll get right to it."

"Mr. Adams—"

"Clint."

"Clint, if we can get the men together fast enough, maybe you and Mr. Diamond can go through some drills with them. I'm not too proud to say I'm not very experienced in guarding banks."

"Clint looked at Diamond who nodded.

"We'll split up into two parties, and Ron and I will each head one up."

"I'll stay with you, and my brother can go with Mr. Diamond. I'll deputize the three of you, but since I'm an unofficial lawman, you'll be unofficial deputies."

"That's fine." Clint turned to McCoy and said, "You'd better tell whoever has a gun to bring it along." To Sean McCoy, he said, "Can you get someone to supply some guns?"

"The general store should be willing. They've got money in the bank, too."

"Better make it rifles. It'll be easier for the men who are not experienced with guns."

"All right."

"Let's get to it," Clint said. "We've got a lot of work to do if we're going to save those banks."

As they walked out of the office, Diamond asked, "What happens if they're planning to hit the payroll as it comes into town?"

"We'll have to allow for that, too. I'll ride out with some men to meet the payroll wagon."

"We will have to find out the route it's taking."

"With McCoy and his brother backing us, I don't think that'll be a problem."

"None of this will be a problem if we're wrong."

"Have you been a pessimist all your life, or is this a recent development?"

Out at the cabin—which was actually within walking distance of town—Doc Lewis took his men through the procedures again, step by step, and then stepped outside for some air. Dan Adams followed him out.

"Everything set with Cord?"

"All set," Lewis said. "He'll go into one bank with four men; we'll take the others. If we can get rid of someone while we're still inside, fine; otherwise we'll wait until we're clear of town. I figure a four-way split."

"You don't figure to try and take Cord, do you?"

"Hell, no," Lewis said. "Let's not get greedy, Dan. We're cutting the split as it is and there's plenty to go around for us four."

"Okay, Doc, whatever you say."

The door opened behind them and Linc Gilmartin walked out.

"I have a question, Doc."

"Go ahead."

"Why not hit the payroll while it's coming into town, before it gets to the bank?"

"We know when it's coming in," Lewis answered, "but we don't know the route. No, we have to wait until it's in the bank."

"And there's no law?"

"Just somebody the loggers assigned to keep the peace. He's not an experienced lawman."

"So there shouldn't be a posse."

"Of what? Loggers? They know almost as much about horses as they do about guns. No, once we're clear of town, we should be free and clear."

"Sounds good to me, Doc."

"I'm glad you approve."

"There's one thing you should know about Henderson, though."

"What's that?"

"He got in some trouble a short time ago. It may catch up to him."

"Did you know about that when you got here?"

"I suspected."

"You have any objection to us taking care of him?"

Gilmartin shrugged and said, "Do what you've got to do . . . as long as I get my share."

"Okay."

Gilmartin turned and went back inside.

"What do you think?"

"I think whatever trouble his friend got into, he probably got him into it. I think," Doc Lewis said, "I'm gonna put a bullet into that one myself."

For the remainder of the fourteenth, the bank robbers drilled out at the cabin—with Lewis, Adams, Burke, and Cord having their own little drill in private—while in town, Clint and Diamond tried to whip a bunch of ill-armed, inexperienced loggers into something resembling a force that could protect the two banks.

Counting Clint, Diamond, Hendry, and the McCoy brothers, they had a force of twenty-one men, and Clint had his doubts about their ability to stand off seven or more experienced outlaws and gunhands. Still, it was all they had to work with.

Clint took nine men over to the Hell's Crossing Bank, while Diamond took ten men across the street to the Loggers' Bank & Trust.

The plan was to let the robbers enter the bank—because later they'd have to prove to a territorial judge that they had acted within the law. It was when the men came out of the bank that they would take action. Both Clint and Diamond decided that most of their force would be deployed on the rooftops. Firing down at the bank robbers from above, they should be able to hit something, even if it was the robbers' horses.

At the end of the day, Clint and Diamond—having instructed their men to meet at the banks at seven in the morning—met with the two logging camp leaders, Rifkin and Ketchum, to arrange to meet with the payroll wagon coming in.

"Diamond will stay in town," Clint explained, "while the McCoy brothers and I take a few men out to meet the wagon and escort it in. Once it's here, and the payroll is unloaded, we'll just wait for the bank robbers to make their move."

"What if they have someone watching?" Ketchum asked. "Won't they be tipped off?"

"That's why we're having the men meet at the bank at seven, before it opens. If they have someone watching, all he'll see is a half dozen men escorting the wagon in. He'll also see those men leave after the money is unloaded."

Both Rifkin and Ketchum seemed satisfied with the plan, although they wished they had more men of Clint and Diamond's experience on hand.

"We have one other experienced man," Clint told them, meaning Hendry, "but he won't help for free."

They'd had this conversation with Hendry already. If he were going to be party to saving the payroll, he wanted to be paid.

"A man's got to make a living, old chaps," he'd said.

"How much does he want?"

"That'll be between you and him. As long as he is assured of something, he'll help."

Rifkin and Ketchum exchanged glances and then agreed.

"At least, we'll have three experienced men."

Both Rifkin and Ketchum were old logging men who knew next to nothing about guns, and it was agreed that they wouldn't be expected to be part of the force guarding the banks. They had logging camps to run.

"That's fine," Clint had said, "I just hope you'll have a payroll to run them with after tomorrow."

TWENTY-EIGHT

They escorted the payroll wagon in without incident. Clint figured that the robbers must not have known the route the wagon was taking, which meant that they probably had no inside information.

Once the payroll was split between the two banks, Clint and the McCoys left and went to Sean McCoy's office.

In the office McCoy poured three cups of coffee and asked, "Why not put the whole payroll in one bank?"

"Two reasons," Clint said. "One, everything has to look normal. If they go into one bank and find no payroll, they'll know something is wrong. It's bad enough that they're experienced and we're not; we don't need them tipped off."

"And the other reason?"

"I've dealt with bankers before," Clint said. "Which banker do you think would give up his portion of the payroll?"

Sean McCoy grimaced and said, "Neither."

"What do we do now?" the other McCoy asked.

"Now," Clint said, walking to the window, "we just wait."

By now Diamond's men should have been deployed on the

rooftops of one bank, while Hendry should have Clint's men placed over the other.

It was time to wait.

Doc Lewis, Burke, Cord, Gilmartin, and Killerman played poker while they were waiting for time to pass. The others just sat and waited—Henderson more nervous than the rest.

As he had stated before, Lewis decided that Henderson would stay by the horses. The nine-man force would ride into town in three groups of three so as not to attract too much attention. By the time anyone noticed the nine horses standing in one place, it'd be too late to do anything.

As one o'clock approached, Lewis threw in the cards and stood up.

"Anybody got any questions?" No one did.

"All right, there's one last thing to consider. I don't want anyone getting trigger-happy, but if anyone does have to fire, it better be to kill someone. You get my meaning? Don't use it unless it's absolutely necessary and then make it count. Understand?"

Everyone nodded.

"I'll kill the first man who fires an unnecessary shot." Everybody looked at each other, but no one said a word. "All right, let's get ready."

"This may be it," Clint said.

"What's happening?" Sean McCoy asked. He nudged his brother awake and moved to the window.

"About ten minutes ago three men rode in. Now three more, and they've put their horses in the same place."

"Where'd they go?"

"The saloon, the general store—none of them went too far from the banks."

"Think there'll be more?"

"We'll have to wait and see. Either these six will start moving toward the bank, or they'll wait for some others."

As Sean McCoy and Clint watched, fifteen minutes passed and another three men rode in.

"Three more," Sean McCoy said.

"All right," Clint said, "it's more than we thought, but I can't see there being more. Nine should be the limit. They'll probably go four and four, with one man by the horses."

As they watched, Sean McCoy realized that Clint Adams knew exactly what he was talking about. Four men started to move toward the Hell's Crossing bank, while four others drifted across the street to the Loggers'. A ninth man was standing by the horses.

"Are any of them your men?"

"Can't tell from here."

As they watched the men enter the banks, Clint hoped that Ron Diamond would be able to control his thirst for revenge.

It was Diamond who spotted the man first. He could see the scar on the man's face as he crossed the street to the Loggers' bank. Diamond knew he'd have to get off the roof and across the street to the other bank if he were going to have his revenge.

The tellers in the bank had been alerted, as were the bank managers, so everything went smoothly inside. There were customers in each bank, but at the sight of the guns, they did what they were told.

Too easy, Doc Lewis was thinking as he cleaned out the vault in the Hell's Crossing bank, it's going too easy—but then he'd planned it that way, so why shouldn't it go off without a hitch?

In the Loggers' bank, Linc Gilmartin's heart was racing.

He watched as Burke filled bag after bag with money, and now he knew another reason Doc Lewis had wanted so many men. With less, they would have had to leave some of the money behind.

"Here," Burke said, handing Gilmartin a large sack stuffed with money. Jesus, Gilmartin thought, if there were eight sacks in all, that meant that a whole sack would be his cut.

Cord, in the Loggers' bank with Burke, Gilmartin, and Hansen, kept his eyes on the latter two men. The first chance he got he'd gun one down and take care of the other later, but he had to make it look good. As Lewis said, the first man who fired an unnecessary shot.

Next to Henderson, Hansen was the most nervous of the bunch, so Cord figured it wouldn't take much to touch him off.

Cord moved close to the man and said, "Watch that teller in window two. I think he's going to try to pull something."

Hansen watched the teller intently, and Cord knew that he'd set the two most nervous men in the building on each other. The teller noticed Hansen watching him and began to sweat.

It was only a matter of time.

"Let's go," Clint said to the McCoys, "but easy. We don't want to spook the man holding the horses."

The three men eased out of Sean McCoy's office and started moving toward the banks. Sean would join the men at the Hells' Crossing, while McCoy and Clint went to the Loggers'.

It was about to come off, and he only hoped it came off right.

"All right," Doc Lewis said, "let's go."

"Got it all?" Adams asked. He was timing the action, but Lewis seemed to have a clock in his head.

"Enough," Lewis said, looking at Perry. The man was cool, so he wouldn't be able to find a reason to kill him in the bank. He'd have to take care of him later. "Let's go."

"On time," Cord said to Burke. "Let's move."

"But there's more," Gilmartin argued.

Cord turned to Gilmartin, watch in hand, and said, "It's time to go."

Gilmartin eyed the vault greedily and said, "All right, I'll cover you."

"Let's move," Cord said.

At that moment, the nervous teller couldn't take it anymore. He started to make a move—whether for a gun or just to run, Cord didn't know—but it was enough for Hansen. He drew his gun in one convulsive movement and fired. The bullet caught the teller in the chest, killing him instantly.

"Hansen," Cord said, and as the man turned, Cord drew and fired, killing him.

"Pick up his sack," Cord told Burke, and for the big man, it was no hardship to carry one more bag.

Gilmartin wasn't stupid. He knew that if he went out first he'd likely catch one in the back.

"I'll cover you," he said again.

"Sure," Cord said. "You first, Burke."

Burke went out, and Cord backed out after him, keeping a wary eye on Gilmartin. As Cord went out the door, Gilmartin, consumed by greed, moved back toward the vault for the rest of his money.

His greed saved his life.

As Clint watched, he saw that whoever had planned this

job had planned it well. As two men came out of the Loggers' Bank with sacks, four men exited the Hell's Crossing Bank at the same moment.

There had been two shots, but the men had been instructed not to react to any shots that took place inside the banks. They had to wait until the men came out. Now that they were, it was time for Sean McCoy to earn the extra money he was making as unofficial sheriff.

"All right, you men," McCoy shouted, "stop right there. You're under arrest."

Henderson, already more nervous than he had ever been, turned in the direction of the voice and fired one shot.

That started the war.

The men on the roof, some of them armed with shotguns, others with rifles, began to fire down at the bank robbers. Clint, on the ground, drew his gun but held his fire. The bank robbers all began to fire back and with considerably more accuracy.

It was obvious from the beginning that the loggers were woefully inept with guns. It would be up to Clint, Diamond, and Hendry to make sure that this thing came out the way it was planned.

It was Diamond who killed Henderson, soon after the man had fired the first shot. Hendry killed Steve Perry as he ran for his horse. Burke took a portion of somebody's buckshot in his right shoulder, but kept moving toward the horses.

"We've got to reach the horses," Doc Lewis shouted. "They'll give us cover."

"Cover my ass," Chris Cord said to himself. The whole thing had gone bad, and he was getting out.

While the other men all tried to reach their horses, Cord slipped around the side of the bank, carrying one sack of money. If he had to, he'd escape on foot while the fight went on in the street.

Of the bank robbers, Doc Lewis, Dan Adams, Bob Killerman, and Dave Burke were left in the street. Earl Hansen was dead in one of the banks; Henderson and Perry were dead in the street. Chris Cord was trying to find a horse, or a way out on foot, while Linc Gilmartin was still inside the Loggers' Bank, filling another sack. He heard the shooting outside and knew he'd have to go out the back way. The people in the bank were simply staying out of his way.

Seeing that there were only four men left in the center of the street, Ron Diamond made his move. The man with the scar had not come out of the Loggers' Bank, so Diamond was going to go in after him.

"McCoy, can you handle this?" Clint asked.

"Sure, there are only four of them. Where are you going?"

"I recognized somebody," Clint said. "I'll be back."

Clint hadn't quite believed it, but he had recognized Chris Cord, the man known as the Rattler. Cord didn't hire out for banks; he hired out to kill people. From the shots they'd heard in one of the banks, Clint assumed that Cord had been hired to cut down on the amount of shares. When the shooting had started, he'd seen Cord slip around the side of the Loggers' Bank, and he moved now to try to intercept him.

Dave Burke caught another load of buckshot, this one in the left thigh. He went down on his ass, bleeding from shoulder and thigh, holding his sack of money and firing back at the roof.

Doc Lewis got on the back of a horse and started to ride toward the end of town. Taylor Hendry, seeing this, began running from rooftop to rooftop, trying to keep pace until he had a clear shot. Finally he ran out of roofs, took aim, and fired at Lewis' retreating back. The bullet caught Lewis square in the back and threw him off his horse. He was dead before he hit the ground.

Dan Adams saw Hendry standing at the edge of a roof, took aim, and fired, striking Hendry in the stomach. The Englishman went down and rolled into a fetal position, waiting for the pain.

There were five horses on the ground, victims of the loggers' bullets, and finally someone caught Bob Killerman with a shot through the throat. Later, several men would claim that it was their bullet that killed him.

Dan Adams, seeing Killerman and Lewis go down, and Burke on the ground, tossed his hands up in the air to give up. The inexperienced loggers, however, did not read his movements correctly and kept firing. Adams went down in a hail of bullets, and Sean McCoy began to call for everyone to stop firing.

Clint circled behind the entire street of buildings on the Loggers' Bank side and decided that if he were Cord, he'd head for the livery. He reached there only moments after Cord, who was actually caught trying to decide between Duke and Satan.

"If you try to get on the big one, he'll stomp you to death."

Cord turned around and immediately recognized Clint.

"The Gunsmith? Here? What the hell are you doing in this joke of a town?"

"Right now I'm stopping you from robbing a bank, Cord."

"You want to try me, Adams?" Cord said. "This is something I've thought about a lot."

"Put the sack down."

Cord dropped the money to his feet, and his arms to his sides.

"The Rattler or the Gunsmith," Cord said. "I wonder how many people have debated who's faster."

"Don't flatter yourself, Cord. You're not even in my class."

Cord's eyes narrowed and he went for his gun, anxious to prove Clint wrong.

He didn't.

Gilmartin was climbing out a back window of the Loggers' Bank, dragging two sacks of money and cursing the bank for not having a back door.

"Drop the sacks," Ron Diamond told him.

"Shit," Gilmartin said. He turned, the neck of a sack grasped in each hand. "Look, friend, why don't you take one? One for you and one for me, that sound fair?"

"I only want one thing from you."

"What's that?"

"I want you to tell me you remember a woman in Canaan, New Mexico."

Gilmartin grinned immediately. "You're the husband?"

"That's right."

"The storekeeper?"

"Right again."

Gilmartin dropped the sacks and said, "You came a long way to die, storekeeper."

Gilmartin went for his gun, but before he could reach it, something punched him in the chest. He fell onto the sacks of money, his blood staining them, and Ron Diamond stood over him and said, "Wrong."

TWENTY-NINE

Of the nine bank robbers, only one remained alive, and that one had buckshot in his shoulder and thigh. They carried him to Sean McCoy's office and locked him in a room in the back.

"I need a doctor," he complained.

"That's rough," McCoy said, "because we don't have one."

"Hey, I'll bleed to death!"

McCoy threw him some rags and said, "Do the best you can."

Sean McCoy came out into his office and found his brother, Clint Adams, and Ron Diamond waiting for him.

"He won't bleed to death. Somebody was using the wrong size buckshot."

"He'll keep until you can get a marshal to come and pick him up," Clint said.

"What was the damage?" Sean asked.

"Three loggers dead," his brother said, "one from Ketchum's and two from Rifkin's. Couple of others got shot up, but they'll be okay."

Sean looked at Clint, and the Gunsmith said, "They won't have to pay Taylor Hendry."

"I'm sorry," Sean said.

"So am I."

McCoy looked at Diamond and said, "Did you get your man?"

"One of them," Diamond said, "the one with the scar. He's behind the bank."

"There's one out in the street with an old shoulder wound not fully healed yet," Sean McCoy said.

"Then that'll be the other one," Ron Diamond said, but oddly enough he did not feel cheated.

"Then it's all over for you," McCoy said.

"For all of us," Diamond said.

"I'm glad for you, my friend," McCoy said. "Now you can go back to your life."

"My life," Diamond said. He looked at Clint and said, "I'll see you in the saloon."

"By golly, I could use a drink myself," McCoy said.

"We've got some cleaning up to do out there first," Sean McCoy said. "I expect you to help me, deputy."

"Ah, brother," McCoy said, "give you a little power and . . ." The big man turned to Clint and asked, "What will you do now?"

"I guess I'll ride back with Diamond for a bit."

"Do you know where he is headed?"

Thinking of a dark-haired, dark-eyed little girl he said, "I think I do."

"Good luck to both of you, then."

"We'll have a drink in the saloon before we go."

"Fine. See you there."

The two brothers left and Clint moved to the door to follow. It had worked out for everyone but Taylor Hendry. He'd found the Englishman on the roof, barely alive, and he stayed that way long enough to tell Clint to tell Diamond that Satan was his.

"I came a long way to die," Hendry had said then.

"A lot of men did," Clint said, and Hendry had died in his arms.

He didn't know exactly what the future held for Ron Diamond, the Diamond Gun, now that his mission of vengeance was over, but he had a little girl waiting for him to come back, and a new horse to get there on.

At least that was a start.

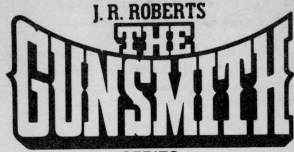

J. R. ROBERTS
THE GUNSMITH

SERIES

Prices may be slightly higher in Canada.